The Truth of Two Lies

Wes Payton

ISBN: 978-1-62420-847-8

Editor: Amanda Armstrong
Cover: Designs by Ms G

Dedication

For my dad, Eugene

Story One: Blind Eye

Chapter One

When I first agreed to do this interview, I thought it was for a podcast, so I figured I could literally phone it in. Apparently, you have to actually show up for a web series. I sit on set, such as it is, waiting for the host to arrive, which frankly feels a bit backwards and a little discourteous, but this is New Media—all the rules have changed, or so I'm told. Is New Media still a term that's used today? Maybe I should read a book about it.

The fledgling talk show host walks on set and sits in the chair opposite mine. He smiles to someone behind the lights. I thought I saw a person moving around back there in the shadows. Certainly, there's no studio audience, since this isn't a studio...more of a storage room that as far as I can tell only stores video equipment, a couple of club chairs upholstered in matching vinyl, and wanton aspirations. The host twirls his finger in the air like an umpire signaling a homerun. I assume the camera is now rolling. Is it still called rolling when it's a digital camera?

The host crosses his legs. "Welcome to our show. Thanks for being with us."

Us? Other than the young woman who let me in, told me where to sit, and then promptly vanished, I haven't seen any evidence of an us. "It's nice to be here with all of you."

"You have a reputation as something of a cantankerous raconteur...in the best possible sense. What's your take on growing older?"

"You mean like a bit? Is your question meant to be a prompt for a routine on aging—that's not really what I do. I'm a humorist...not a comedian—artist, not performing artist."

"Yes, of course...I just thought you might like to share some insights on—"

"You'll edit this part out, right?" I interrupt. "Or maybe we could start again."

"No, I don't think that'll be necessary...let's just press on." The host uncrosses his legs. His polyester suit shines in the spotlight. "You've been writing for over—"

"I never ask anymore what someone's problem is."

"Pardon."

"That's when I first knew I was old. When I was your age, I might ask somebody acting a fool, 'Hey, what's your problem, fella?' But now it's enough for me to know that they clearly have a problem and thus ought to be avoided; it's not my job to identify their problem. These days when I smell shit I don't bother looking around for the source of the odor. I just get up and leave."

The host shuffles the notecards he's holding. "We're known for our bluntness...it's sort of this show's hallmark, you might say, so I hope you don't find this next question impertinent."

He looks at me expectantly. "I hope not either?"

"The first two books in your *Blind Eye* series were quite successful. *Depth of Field* and *Object Permanence* are both beloved by readers the world over; however, your third offering failed to resonate with audiences in the same manner, and now you have a fourth installment in your series that you've been making the rounds to promote."

He looks at me the same way again. "Sorry, did I miss your question? At my age, I sometimes zone out."

"I suppose what I'm attempting to ask is if the last book wasn't a success, why bother with another?"

"Ah...well, the truth is that you write the story you want to tell and then you try pushing it up the hill, because what the hell else are you going to do with it? I saw Sisyphus just the other day, and he says to me, 'I thought I had it tough.'"

"So you'd say being a writer is tougher than, I don't know, being a garbage collector?"

2

"No, I'm not saying that...times are tough all over."

"Why do you think your last book wasn't a success?"

"It wasn't as successful as the first two, but I don't think it was a failure either. I tried to give readers something different... something unexpected."

"Do you think that's what they wanted?"

I rub the back of my neck. "Expectations are a funny thing—sometimes what you think you want may not be what you really want."

"That sounds profound-ish."

"Anyway, the title probably didn't help sales either."

"*The Apparent Trap.*"

"Yeah," I nod. "It seems there's a classic kids movie called something similar."

"And you didn't know that?"

"I...it was mentioned to me early on, but I was dismissive. In retrospect, that might've been an error in judgment on my part."

"There have been those who've speculated that you were aware the third installment was inferior to the first two, and you intentionally entitled it something fatuous, so that if you ever decided to write another in the series, you could blame the poor response to the previous book on the jokey title."

"I think you—or at least those who've been speculating—are giving me too much credit. I'm really not as prescient as all that."

"So what can readers expect from this fourth book—more of the same or something unexpected again? I dare say the title, *Empty Spaces*, sounds rather vacuous."

"Intentionally so," I reply. "I hope it evokes for the reader the vast distances between our atoms, which are connected by strands of energy like a net, but what are we meant to hold in that net exactly?"

"Perhaps nothing."

"Some of us, maybe...the vapid, I suppose."

The host rests his note cards on the arm of his chair. "You write a lot of dialogue."

"That's correct."

"Which some of your readers find off-putting."

"I think they more likely find it down-putting, at which point the people to whom you refer can no longer accurately be classified as my readers."

"It's been suggested that you ought to simply write screenplays instead of novels, since it seems nowadays the mark of a successful book is whether or not it's made into a movie."

"More's the pity."

"Yes, but none of your novels have ever found their way to the silver screen."

"More's the penurious."

"Have you considered turning one of your dialogue-heavy stories into a stage play? I ask, because there's an odor motif that runs through your *Blind Eye* books, which the reader never fully gets to appreciate, just as a moviegoer would likewise miss out on smelling such scents; however, at a theater you could have a prop master in the wings, I don't know, spraying perfumes or burning various spices to release smells into the air that correspond with the fragrances from your stories."

"I'm incensed at your suggestion. I jest...no, that selfsame proposal has been tendered before, but honestly plays always seem a bit stagey to me. On the rare occasion when I attend the theater, I inevitably feel more like I'm there to satisfy the needs of the actors than they're there to satisfy mine. Meanwhile, all the people around me in the audience appear to be seeing something that I'm not, or at least putting on their own performance and pretending to, leaving me feeling like the only one in the congregation who's not sensing the Holy Spirit. People talk about how transformative theater can be, and it makes me wonder what those theatergoers were like before their transformation into snobs who gush pretentious nonsense. Simply put, theater ruins people, and if it's what our culture is going to hang its hat on, then I submit that we just don't deserve to wear a hat."

"Then you're opposed to the idea?"

"Resolutely so...although, it's never a good idea to say never."

The host lets out a long sigh as he consults his note cards once more.

"Don't worry, we'll edit this part out." After a few moments he returns his note cards to the arm of his chair just as they had been before. "I read once that you don't read very much."

"I believe what I said in the print interview to which you're likely referring is that one reads fiction for truth and nonfiction for reality. Finding no truth in contemporary fiction, I prefer to read for reality, though I often find the subject distasteful."

"So then you just don't read novels—why?"

"The themes of novelists writing today aren't worth the time it takes to suss them out. Inevitably, they're either too abstruse, which is probably why they weren't the subjects of essays or some other more straightforward writing in the first place, or they won't stand up on their own so they need to be couched in a multifaceted story that can be endlessly interpreted and thus never clearly understood—just like the Bible—in which case all you're left with is the source material for some future cult."

He flips a card over. "You once said, and I quote: 'The Bible was intentionally designed to be both inscrutable and incoherent, so it could either be used as the basis for an impenetrable contract or a cult's constitution.'"

"Yes, I suppose I did say that—one says a lot of things when one has a career as long and checkered as mine. What your interview style lacks in originality it makes up for in research, I'll give you that."

"Do you often feel as if you have nothing new to say?"

"I'd be more inclined to say something new if I felt people had actually listened to the old things I'd said before."

"Maybe it's not so much that audiences aren't listening but more that they're no longer listening to you."

"Says the talk show host who literally doesn't have an audience."

"I'd wager that my show has been listened to by more people than your last audiobook."

"That's not really a fair comparison...my understanding is that most people play programs like this for the background noise while they're busy doing other things. As far as I can surmise, your show caters to listeners who're too preoccupied to actually listen."

The host rolls his eyes. "Let's shift gears, shall we? You started out as a mystery writer. If you were going to murder someone in real life, how would you do it?"

"If I had a mind to torture them to death, I'd have them come here."

"I wanted to like you. How come I don't?"

"I'm as divisive as black licorice."

"I had hopes that you'd become a friend of the show—a regular guest."

"Anything is possible, though I know people usually mean that in a good way."

The host turns a final card. "I have one last question for you."

"What're you trying to do, write a thesis or something? I do happen to think you're correct about one thing."

"What's that?"

"Nothing...I just wanted your attention so that I could ask you a question—do you smell something?" I rise to leave. "Perhaps you can come by the theater when we open so the prop master can hook you up to the ventilation system for that pivotal outhouse scene."

The host tosses his cards into the air. "All's well that ends well."

"Well, we all die in the end, so I'm not too sure about that."

Chapter Two

I walk to the old neighborhood a few blocks down from the so-called studio. I slide into my old bar and my feet stick. How could anyone sweep a floor this sticky? The burly bartender looks up from his cellphone as I mount a stool.

"I remember you...don't get many white guys in here these days—at least not old ones."

"The complexion of this bar may've changed, but not the character. I used to let a room upstairs—living beyond my means whilst living in a shitty, studio apartment with cockroaches for roommates. One night I awoke to what I thought were gunshots, but it turned out only to be fireworks."

"Right, I think you said that last time too. Didn't you tell me you were a writer. Can't you afford a nicer bar than this one?"

"Sure, but they can't afford me."

"How's that?"

"Bars are places where one buys overpriced booze to pay for a vomit-receptacle of a venue and the company of an inattentive bartender whose only apparent qualification for his job is that he's not qualified to do anything else."

"I see what you mean...upscale joint would probably find that sort of talk offensive to its clientele."

I scan the empty stools and tables. "Whereas you have no clientele to offend."

"It's early yet, and I wouldn't suggest that sort of loose talk when my clientele does start to roll in. So what can I get you? We ain't got no frou-frou shit."

"In that case I'll have your best bourbon on the rocks."

7

"We can do that."

I look up at the television hanging from the ceiling and catch a glimpse of a music video. "Why's that guy still have the price tag hanging from his baseball cap."

The bartender turns to look as he fills a glass with ice. "He's a rapper...it's the style."

"Was for Minnie Pearl, too."

"This is the song for that new Wenzel Lincoln movie—play it all the time on this channel."

"World's most famous black actor, and he's got a gun in almost every picture he makes...yeah, our culture is in great shape."

"Lincoln plays a cop from the future in this one." He sets the glass in front of me and pours the booze. "I'm gonna go see it tonight with my girl."

"Well, I sincerely hope you two don't get shot by a ray gun." My mobile phone vibrates in my pocket, and I check who's calling. "It's my agent. Do you mind turning that crap down?"

The bartender shrugs. "It's rap—not crap."

"Same difference." I flip open my phone.

"How'd the taping go?"

"I don't think they call it that anymore. Everything's digital nowadays—no tape."

"Fine, how'd the podcast go? Please tell me you didn't call in with your TV blaring in the background."

"No, it was a web series or whatever. I had to go down to this storage unit to do it—stank of mildew and mediocrity."

"Oh...I swear they said podcast when I called to book you."

"You called them?"

"Yeah, it's been a while since you've done any press, so I wanted you to get a running start."

"I don't know about at the start, but I definitely felt like running by the end."

"Then I take it that it didn't go so well...good."

"Good?" I ask.

"I was hoping you'd get all that curmudgeonly crud you've been building up over the last couple of years out of your system."

"But I doubt they'll even broadcast my segment."

"I think you mean upload...and who cares? The important thing is that you're in fine fettle for your spot on that late-night talk show tomorrow, which actually will be televised."

"I don't like the new host they've got. What happened to the old one?"

"He retired; he's doing his own web series now...or maybe a podcast, I can't remember which."

"Could you call him to book me on that then? I'm sure he'd have me on for old time's sake."

"You'd think so, but I believe his new program is more youth oriented—the gimmick being that an avuncular grump interviews artists who are up-and-coming."

"Not down-and-out." I take a sip of bourbon. "Maybe I should start my own podcast. I'm an avuncular grump."

"Well, you're half right, but let's stay focused on getting audiences to read your words rather than listen to them. Anyway, don't drink too much today. I want you rested for your interview tomorrow; you don't sleep off the booze as well as you once did."

"Thanks for the vote of confidence."

"I'm confident that the cleared-eyed version of you can still sell a lot of books...do something to stretch your brain this afternoon and then go home and get a good night's rest."

"I was thinking of going to see the Damon Hearst exhibit that just came to town."

"Don't think about it—do it...then go out for a big dinner and after that straight to bed sans nightcap."

"But how will I keep my head warm?"

"A cool head is what I'm hoping for during your interview—not an irritable writer who's hot under the collar. You aged out of your angry young man years some time ago."

"I'm hanging up now."

"Fine, but I'll be watching tomorrow night—do us proud."

I return the phone to my pocket and finish off the last of my bourbon.

"Want another?" asks the bartender.

"No, one will do it today—agent's orders."

Chapter Three

What's black and white and gilded all over? A golden-hoofed zebra suspended in a 10,000-gallon fish tank filled with formaldehyde. Jesus, art makes so much sense these days. How about an exhibit of smoldering rubble where this museum used to be—that'd make for an incendiary installation.

You may be asking why I even came here...just to be irritated? Honestly, I'm not sure. I don't understand this world anymore, but sometimes I still feel like I need to see it for myself. I walk around the tank, dodging the swarm of museumgoers taking selfies with the cadaver. The lid of the tank must not be on tight; I'd swear I can smell the acrid odor of embalming fluid.

As I ponder how nowadays art museums aren't so much in on the joke, but rather are the joke, I notice in my peripheral vision this purple guy sidling up next to me...I know, purple—we can hold hands if you want so that we get there together.

"How much do you think something like that costs?" he asks me.

"Way more than I've made in my lifetime."

"And how much poverty is there in this world?"

"A lot more than a little."

"This displeases me."

I nod. "I'm not exactly doing cartwheels over it either."

"I create something as uniquely beautiful as a zedra, and you people take it from its home and put it on display in a gaudy glass box."

"I think you mean zebra, and what's with the 'you people'? For someone who seems to want me to believe that he's omniscient, you don't listen so well."

The man grins. "I'm surprised you aren't nonplussed by my

appearance. Do you have many plum-colored people in this world?"

"Not since we extirpated all the Aubergines and Heliotropes some years ago. Also, since none of these people snapping pictures around us have bothered to take a photo of you, I'm pretty sure you're not real."

"What's that say about you then?"

"That I've very likely gone insane, but then to hear my agent tell it—with the talent comes the crazy."

"Do you want to touch me?"

"Fuchsia's not my type."

The man grins again. "No, I mean to prove to you that I'm real."

"How would that prove anything? I can already see and hear you...corroborating your existence with a third of my five senses wouldn't change all that much."

"No, I suppose not. Do you mind if we talk someplace less crowded?"

"How about the statuary courtyard? It's my favorite area of the museum as it's mostly overlooked."

We walk through the portraiture gallery. A guard admonishes a young lady for using a flash to take a picture of an oil painting depicting a stern-looking woman with a scepter. Off with her head!

As we approach the garth, he steps behind me when a gaggle of unruly schoolchildren exits the very door we intend to enter. It seems I'm meant to be his blocker against the tide of children. Having made our way through the field trippers, I open the door for him, and we step onto the crushed limestone pathway. As we walk toward an armless marble statue, I abruptly halt. His shoes don't make the same crunching noise on the gravel as mine; in fact, his footfalls don't make any sound at all.

"Clever," he says. "Inside I was prepared to send a signal to your brain if you had chosen to touch me, but I was unprepared for the change in the surface on which we now walk."

"So you are in my head then."

"In a manner of speaking, but I assure you that I'm not a figment of your imagination. If anything, you're a figment of mine."

"You're telling me that you've imagined my entire existence? What barren dreams you must have."

"No, I imagined the possibility of you...of your whole world, and then I took steps to create this reality. I promise, you're quite real, as am I. We just don't happen to occupy the same reality. We exist in different dimensions. The atoms that I'm comprised of exist in those empty spaces between the atoms that you're comprised of, although at slight variations in space-time. Skin color notwithstanding, our most salient dissimilarity is that one of us learned long ago to manipulate those variations."

"Okay."

He tilts his lavender head. "Okay?"

"Okay, and..."

"And what?"

"There're over eight billion people on this planet. Why are you talking with me?"

"Ah, well, I'm afraid I have some rather distressing news. It's my intention to end this world very soon."

"Okay."

"I must say, I'm surprised at my utter inability to surprise you."

"Don't take it personally. I've been depressed for the past several decades. They tell me it'll pass. Another decade or so and I think they'll be proven correct. In the fog of depression, bad news tends not to be all that surprising."

He points to a stone bench. "Do you mind if we have a seat? I'm not accustomed to standing so much."

"I thought—"

"I'm doing all the things, walking and talking, that the me you see is doing; I'm just doing them in another dimension, and in that dimension I almost never stand for this long. It's hard on my knees."

"I know what you mean." We both take a seat on the bench. "So why do you want to destroy this world?"

"I find it interesting that 'why' and not 'how' is your first question."

"I'm an erstwhile mystery writer. Motive is more important to me than method...and don't think I've forgotten that you've yet to answer my previous 'why' question about why you're talking to me."

"In point of fact, they're both related. I've decided to do away with this world because I've grown bored with it—have been for quite a while...time to make space for something new."

"I know just how you feel, but again what's that got to do with me?"

"Well, as a citizen of this world, my decision directly impacts you."

"Right, but how come I get the advanced notice?"

"Because, simply put, you interest me."

I shake my head. "I've known me my whole life, and I promise I'm not all that interesting."

"I quite agree, but the new book you've written is very much of interest to me."

"My book...it's not even out yet."

"I'm an interdimensional being, you landlubber. Do you think I really need to wait in line at a bookstore to read a copy?"

"Shows what you know—there aren't lines at bookstores anymore...there are hardly even bookstores."

He rests his hands on his knees. "That's the gist of it, really. I've read all your books—don't be overly flattered, I read most everything. Nothing, written or otherwise, in any reality is denied to me, and it's all so dull, but in this new book of yours you capture something...interesting, so I'm interested to learn if your fellow humans will pick up on it."

"Trust me, they won't. My last book was an abysmal failure, so no one's in a hurry to pick up my new one."

"They don't have to be in a hurry. I'll give them a week."

The color begins to drain from his face, and a moment later I'm looking at the transparent version of him. I reach out to touch his nose; it feels firm but somehow not real, as if my fingertip is pressing against an unyielding idea in my head. He winks at me and then disappears completely.

My phone vibrates in my pocket. It's a most unexpected caller.

Chapter Four

An hour later I'm knocking on the front door of the house that belongs to my daughter-in-law-ish. I always hated standing on this porch, surrounded as it is by the cloying stench of irises. The door opens. "Iris, I was surprised to get your call."

"I know...I bet you're thinking I only call when I need something."

"Or not at all. It's been a while."

"The phone works both ways, you know."

"I'm an old man. What do I have to talk about...my prostate?"

She slips into a pair of heels in the foyer. I notice her dangling earrings. She never used to wear but more than one piece of jewelry, which is missing from her left hand. "Thanks again for agreeing to watch him on such short notice."

"Sure...you mentioned on the phone that you have a pressing appointment. Is it a job interview or something?"

"Did I say appointment?"

"Yes."

"Well, it's more like a date, which I believe is a type of appointment, if you think about it."

"I shall try not to."

"My therapist told me that tonight is an important milestone, but if this doesn't feel like the right time, then I can cancel. It's just that I've...we've been looking forward to this for weeks, but then my babysitter—"

I raise my hands. "For me it doesn't so much feel like the right time but rather my last opportunity. I want to see my grandson again before I shuffle off this mortal coil."

"Okay...but could you not say stuff like that around him? He's kind of a sensitive boy."

"Having a father who commits suicide will do that to a kid."

"Or stuff like that. We haven't really talked about what happened to Daddy yet."

"It's been almost two years."

She nods. Her earrings dither. "I know how long it's been."

"Is he housebroken yet? Last time I saw him, he was still in diapers."

"Yes, he's five, so he's fully potty trained...and he's a boy, not a puppy."

"Sometimes I forget since his mother is such a bitch."

"We never really did have a talk about...the things that happened."

"You mean trying to divorce my suicidal son."

"I only married into the family. You're the one he got his saturnine genes from, so you should know that I'm still pissed about that. Anyway, we're both here now, but are you sure you're up for babysitting tonight? I have reservations—"

"At a dog park?"

"About leaving my son with his grandad if he's been drinking. Your breath smells vaguely of booze."

"I had one drink with lunch."

"Did you have any lunch with lunch? There's mac and cheese in the microwave." A car horn honks, and she glances furtively over my shoulder. "I should get going. We have reservations—"

"At a kennel?"

"At a restaurant downtown. The number is on the fridge if something comes up."

"Aren't you going to reintroduce me to my grandson first?"

"He's watching his favorite show. He wouldn't notice you now if I introduced you as Santa Claus, but we had a talk after I called you. We looked at the photo album, and I reminded him of who you are. Just feed him dinner when his show's over and then make sure he brushes his teeth before bed."

"Okay, I was probably going to eat mac and cheese tonight anyway. It'll be nice to have the company...whenever he's done watching television."

She stands up tall in her heels and hugs me. "Believe it or not, I've missed you." Then those heels clack across the foyer tile toward the waiting sedan.

~ * ~

I check the mac and cheese in the microwave. The cellophane has already been perforated and the cardboard sleeve carefully set on the countertop below with the heating instructions facing up. Back in my day, growing boys ate...oh, forget it.

I round the corner into the living room. "Hey champ, you remember me?"

The boy moves his head in my direction but not his eyes; they stay trained on the TV. "Yeah, Mommy showed me some pictures."

I move to block the screen. It's always been my policy to meet them where they are. "Whatcha watching?"

He moves his head again, and this time his eyes move too so they can see around the obstruction. "Barney."

"The purple dinosaur? I didn't know he was still on." Then I notice adult voices emanating from the television. I turn and realize he's watching *Barney Miller*. "Your mom lets you watch this?"

"She likes it too."

"Sure, but...is this a DVD?"

He seems confused. "We stream it."

"Then can you pause it? I'd like to talk with you for a few minutes."

He reluctantly picks up the remote from the sofa cushion and points it at the TV. Hal Linden's face becomes frozen in a half blink. His mustache has never looked better.

I take a seat on the sofa. "I thought I'd order us a pizza for dinner. What toppings do you like?"

"I thought we were having mac and cheese."

"You'd rather have that than pizza? When I was your age pizza—"

"Yes."

"Yes?"

He nods at me as if he thinks I might be deaf. "Yes, I want mac and cheese instead of pizza."

"Oh, all right. Do you want me to make it now?"

"Can I finish my show first?"

"Why do you like *Barney Miller* so much?"

"I don't know." As if to emphasize his point for the hard of hearing, he shrugs.

"I used to like this show because all the characters wanted to make the best of a bad situation; it made dealing with criminals all day seem kind of funny, so maybe the rest of the world is kinda funny too. If you tell me why you like it, I'll let you get back to your show while I go nuke us some dinner."

"I like the way Barney takes care of everybody. Daddy was like that, wasn't he?"

I've always been in favor of saving one's tears for the shower; I've been keeping pretty clean these past couple years. Not wanting to weep like a silly old man in front of the boy, I tousle his hair and tell him dinner will be ready whenever he is.

~ * ~

I wake up on the couch when I hear heels in the foyer. I can tell she's been crying. Women are silly that way. "How'd the date go?"

She steps out of her pointy shoes and takes a seat on the recliner. "Dinner was lovely, but I think my shrink was wrong...it seemed too soon, so we're just going to stay friends."

"Exactly what every guy wants to hear after shelling out for a fancy meal."

"I split the check with him."

"You really are out of practice when it comes to dating."

"How'd you two spend your evening?"

I stifle a yawn. "Watched a *Barney Miller* marathon—actually saw an episode that didn't entirely take place at the police station."

"Did you get him to brush his teeth before bed? You have to insist."

"I don't feel as if I know the boy well enough to make demands of him."

She rolls her eyes. "Do you want to sleep here tonight? I can make up the couch."

"No, I'll just call a cab."

"Call a cab...people still do that? The least I can do is order you up an Uber."

"If you insist."

Chapter Five

The streetlights slip past faster as the driver accelerates onto the expressway. I watch the movie of my day flicker on the window of the rear passenger's side door. I've talked to more people today than I usually talk to in a month—the ascetic life of an aesthete. You'd think all I'd want to do now is go home to be by myself.

I lean forward. "Can you take me to a tavern in Old Towne?"

The driver turns his head slightly toward me. "Sorry, I've got to drop you where the app says."

"I'll give you fifty bucks."

"Old Towne isn't a destination I would've accepted this time of night."

"Make it a hundred."

"Cash?"

"No, make believe money." I hand him a C-note.

"Okay mister, give me the address so I can find the directions on my phone."

~ * ~

I slide into the old bar again. It's considerably more crowded than before. I take a seat atop one of the few open stools.

"You sure you're in the right place, pops?"

"I come here all the time—earlier today, in fact. The barman on then told me he was going tonight to see that new sci-fi cop movie." I point to the TV. "The one this rap video is for."

The bartender glances up at the television. "Okay old timer, I don't need your life story. I just want to make sure you know where you are. So what can I get you?"

"Bourbon on the rocks—not that stuff from under the bar either...reach for the high shelf."

The bartender pulls down a brown bottle. "Hey, it's your call."

After the bartender leaves for the other end of the bar, I take a long swig, not giving the ice a chance to melt away the smoky burn. I set my drink down, and the ice cubes rattle around in the mostly empty glass.

"Long day?" asks the mauve man suddenly sitting beside me.

"Oh, it's you again. I was wondering when you'd reappear."

"Then I take it you've been thinking about our conversation from earlier today."

"Among other things."

"Care to share your thoughts?"

I finish off the last of the bourbon. "My working theory is that I'm dead, and I just don't know it yet."

"Given your lifestyle, I can see how you'd arrive at that conclusion, but I don't think ghosts drink."

"Really, what makes you say that?"

"Because they don't exist."

"How do you know?"

"Like I told you before, I'm an interdimensional being older than the world as you know it. If there were any dimension occupied by spectral apparitions, I would've encountered them by now."

"Some things you have to take on faith."

I raise my empty glass and the bartender returns.

"That was fast—you must've been thirsty."

"Still am...I'll have another and one for my friend here too."

The bartender looks at the empty stool next to mine. "I don't think you got no friends in this place, old timer. I tell you what, I'll make this one a double for ya, and when you finish it, you'd better call it a night."

The bartender refills my glass nearer to the brim and walks off.

This time I give the ice and whiskey a moment to make their

acquaintances. "So, you're both intangible and invisible—except to me. How'd I get so lucky?"

"We share a connection. You can see and feel me in your mind, if I so choose it."

"That seems like a rather one-sided connection. Why can't I pop up into your empurpled dimension?"

"I come from a considerably more advanced race of beings who perfected interdimensional travel. My ancestors didn't waste so much time warring as yours."

"I always thought the one positive side effect of war was advancement."

"Sure, for your benighted civilization. You people would've advanced a lot further had you focused more on ending wars than winning them."

I'm ready for that drink now. "As they say, hindsight's 20/20."

"That would prove helpful, if only time weren't linear."

"You mean you can jump from dimension to dimension, but you can't swim against the flow of the timestream?"

"I'm afraid not."

"Then what good are you, eggplant?"

A patron two stools down leans back to get a better look at me. "Who're you calling an eggplant, you old cracker?"

I wave my hand dismissively. "Sorry, I was speaking to someone else."

The man stands up. "Somebody else...sitting in an empty stool? You were looking right at me."

"My apologies, I must've been talking to myself. I may have been looking in your direction but trust me, I was just staring off into space."

The man takes a step closer. "I don't care if you were talking to the man in the moon. I come here to get away from white people, but tonight I come in and a honky calls me an eggplant."

"Hold on, listen—"

"No, you listen. I grew up near Little Italy, so I know what it means

22

when some old wop says you're an eggplant."

I look to the mauve man, who seems to be enjoying this exchange. "Wait, I'm not even Italian."

"Is that supposed to make it better?"

I raise my hands to protest. He raises his fists for a different reason, takes a swing, belts me in the face, and I fall from my stool. I reflexively touch the throbbing area around my eye.

"Now you'll be the eggplant tomorrow." The patron resumes his barstool.

I stand up and see the bartender approaching. He reaches for my drink. "Time to go."

I grab the glass first and quickly down its contents, then return it to the bar with a hollow thud. "I was just thinking the same thing."

The mauve man follows me out the door into the chilly evening. I pull my jacket tight around me. "I'm gonna have a helluva time finding a cab around here. Can't you give me a lift in your spaceship or something?"

"I find space travel tedious...also, I'm not your guardian angel."

"You're definitely right about that." I wipe blood from under my nose on the streetcorner. "At least I won't have to worry about getting robbed, as it looks like I've already been mugged."

"I'm glad to hear it." The color drains from his skin. "I'll call on you next when you're somewhat less harried."

"Sounds like I'll never see you again."

And he's gone.

Chapter Six

I sit in the greenroom, awaiting my turn to chat with the host. The ingénue from the new Wenzel Lincoln movie gets the first slot—makes sense, she's much prettier than I am, though I watched a couple minutes of her segment, and it didn't seem like she had much to say, which strikes me as a liability for a talk show guest. Then the ball player is up next—nearly seven feet tall and biceps for brains, so not exactly a scintillating conversationalist. Finally, it'll be me...the best for last. The third slot of the evening is typically given to a musical act, which is no doubt what this studio audience would prefer. I suspect even a cooking segment would make for better television than an interview with a washed-up writer; at least there'd be the possibility of a grease fire to enliven the end of this live show.

I stretch out on the red couch. (It occurs to me that no part of this greenroom is actually green—maybe I'll mention that in my segment.) I've done enough of these shows over the years that I don't get nervous the way I used to when I first arrived on the scene, but still...it'd be nice to have someone here with me to help pass the time. There's a knock at the door and a young person pokes his/her head in and tells me, "Five minutes."

I can hardly wait.

I go stand in front of the mirror. My orbital contusion appears flat black, but at least the puffiness has filled in the wrinkles around one of my eyes. I look like the Exxon Valdez crashed into my face. (Maybe I'll use that too, though I suppose it's a pretty dated reference.) I scan the small room in the mirror, thinking I might catch a reflection of the mauve man, but it's as lonely as the inside of a coffin in here.

I exit the greenroom and walk toward the wings of the stage where all is a tumult of whispers and gesticulations. An old woman with

24

headphones points to me and then points to an X comprised of two intersecting strips of electrical tape affixed to the floor near the edge of the curtain. Or is it gaffer's tape? Was that woman a gaffer? Can she be both a gammer and a gaffer? (No one's going to get that; I definitely shouldn't use it.) I take position where I'm told.

During the commercial break, the producer talks to the young host at his desk, I presume to remind him of who I am. The host turns in my direction and smiles at me with obnoxiously white teeth. I nod back. The stage lights come up, and the audience applauds just as the illuminated signs overhead instruct. The host says something I can't quite make out, but it gets a laugh from the audience. Then he waves me on as the audience applauds again, more tepidly this time. I'd feel less uncomfortable being shot out of a cannon.

I walk across the small stage (it looks bigger on TV), engage in a clammy handshake with the host—my hands are mollusked, not his—then take a seat in the empty chair nearest the desk.

"It's good to see you again."

The host takes his seat. "Sorry, have we met before?"

"My mistake, I meant it's good to be here again."

"Right, back in the day you were something of a regular on the old show."

"If the show retains the same name, doesn't that make it the same show?"

"Is the *King Kong* with Fay Wray the same movie as the one with the CGI gorilla?"

"Is your gaffer also a gammer?"

"Do you mean a gamer?"

"No, I don't." I take a sip of water from the coffee mug on his desk. They used to fill it with liquor upon request.

"Anyway, before I jump into my first question, I have to ask—that's quite a shiner you've got there. You know we have a makeup artist on staff, right?"

"Yes, he dropped by backstage, but at my age you tend to feel like a

25

corpse when you wear makeup, so I declined."

"A bold choice." The host looks to the teleprompter. "You've been writing for years—"

"Ever since grammar school."

"Yes, ah...and you're perhaps best known for your Black Eye, er, I mean *Blind Eye* books, but I wanted to ask you about your signature, uh, gimmick for a lack of a better term—the double contraction."

"Right, my great contribution to contemporary literature."

"How did you first come up with the idea? I'd've figured it'd've been thought of long ago."

"I can see on the prompter what you did there. At this point it was thought up long ago, and I'm sure there were other writers who thought it up even before then, but they didn't have the benefit of working with an incompetent editor on their first book, so it became my signature, as you say. Truthfully, double contractions were just something I did to save time and ink ribbons in the days when manual typewriters were still a thing; I always assumed they'd be fixed by the proofreader or somebody, but then my publisher back then never saw a corner unfit for cutting. Anyway, don't underestimate a good gimmick; they're often necessary to get people's attention, even when what you have to say is worthy of their attention."

"That almost sounded poetic."

I chuckle to myself. "That's funny, yesterday I was accused of almost sounding profound."

"You've been a writer for decades. Have you ever tried your hand at writing poetry?"

"Not my hand or any other part of my body, though perhaps I ought to as it seems I might be in need of a new gimmick to hook younger readers."

The host frowns. "I doubt that would do it. Don't get me wrong, I was told you were talented, and you certainly speak well enough, but the world is full of clever people who don't end their sentences with prepositions that the 18- to 34-year-old market just doesn't want to hear from. Some nights I feel like we exclusively book those people on this very show. They sit right where you are now."

"Never let it be said that I'm not a fair man. I appreciate all unsolicited observations equally."

"I always do what I can...and then a little more."

The audience giggles at his remark for reasons that are unclear to me.

"People laugh for many different reasons," I say sotto voce.

"What's that?"

"Oh...I was just reminded of this crawling leper I stepped over on my way in here today. He said he intended to have one last laugh before he died. If he managed to make it into this theater, I think he has a chance of living forever."

"Is that meant to be funny?"

"Not if you're afflicted with leprosy, I suppose."

The host gives me a long stare. "Careful what you say...you might hurt someone's feelings."

"Yes, we should all try being more sensitive. I don't mean toward one another, mind you, but rather about how easily each of us gets offended—that should fix everything."

"You really are the curmudgeon they say, aren't you?"

"From the bottom of that fist-sized organ that occupies the middle of my chest, which beats like clockwork thrice every minute."

The host takes off his wristwatch. "Speaking of clockwork, I understand you're making the rounds hawking this new book of yours. I bet you could sell ice to an Inuit."

"It'd be easier to sell you a less staid analogy, since you're so clearly in need of one."

He hands me his watch. "Here, sell me my Rolex."

"You want me to sell you a timepiece that you already own?"

"Come on—just try...it'll be fun."

"In all good conscience, I can't sell you this timepiece." I let the watch fall to the floor and then crush its crystal face with the heel of my Oxford. "A man of your obvious class and sophistication deserves a Patek Philippe."

"I take it back—that wasn't as much fun as I thought it'd be."

"It seemed like good television to me," says the mauve man who's suddenly seated next to me.

I turn to my right to look at the occupant of the previously empty chair. "Really...now is the less harried time you chose to pop in for a chat? As you can clearly see, I'm already talking with one space case."

"As I told you yesterday, I eschew space travel."

"I'm sorry," says the host, "what's happening here?"

"It seems you're double booked," I explain. "Another guest has arrived, but you can only see him out of the corner of your eye, as he exists on the periphery of perception."

The host stares for a moment at what appears to him to be the empty chair next to mine. "Ah, you've brought an imaginary friend."

"Friend is a bit of an overstatement. I only met him yesterday when he told me that he intends to destroy the world as we know it."

"And how does he plan to do that?"

"I don't know." I shrug and turn to the mauve man. "How do you?"

"I shall release a meteor through my interdimensional portal the same way all those millennia ago that I released the meteor freighted with a genetic payload, which gave rise to life on your then barren planet, though this meteor will be considerably more impactful."

"Okay, got it." I turn back toward the host. "Meteor...big boom."

"That sounds rather unpleasant. Is there any way we can forestall such a calamity?"

"Yes, but it's a bit embarrassing."

"Do tell...it seems the fate of our planet may depend upon it."

"People have to buy my new book...or rather, they don't actually have to buy it, but they have to read it."

"And how many people, exactly?"

"I don't know exactly...all of them, I think."

The host lets out a low whistle. "This is the most ingenious marketing plan I've ever heard of...read my new book or we're all going to die."

"We're all going to die regardless of whether you read my book or not; it's just a matter of timing, if the mauve man is to be believed."

"Ah, he's purple no less." The host slaps his desk. "This man who's sitting beside you that only you can see."

"Yes, he's purple, and I don't know if only I can see him, but apparently you cannot."

"How about it folks?" the host asks the audience. "Can any of you seen this amethyst man?"

I hear laughter interspersed with boos.

The host shakes his head. "Are you sure you didn't get a concussion to go with that bruise."

"No, I saw the mauve man before I got this violet badge."

"Your new book, *Empty Spaces*, is the fourth in the series. Why parade out this promotional gambit now? Why not for the underperforming previous one, or perhaps the first in the series?"

"You play the cards your dealt. I wasn't seeing purple people eaters back then."

"So he eats people now?"

"He's incorporeal, so cannibalism is beyond his capacity. I was being hyperbolic, as is a writer's wont."

"Thank goodness for small favors."

"And this isn't a publicity stunt to drum up books sales. I'm an old man and by no means a man of means...I may not have Rolex money, but I have enough money to live out the rest of my life comfortably, so at this point I don't really care how many books I sell."

"I see...would you mind asking this amethyst man a question for me? That is my job after all."

"You can ask him yourself. He can see and hear you—just not the reverse...at least I think that's correct." I turn to my right. "That's correct, isn't it?"

The mauve man nods. "Quite so."

I turn back to my left. "Yes, that's right—ask away."

The host clears his throat. "I don't make it a habit of talking to people I can't see or hear but let me start by saying welcome to Earth."

The mauve man rolls his dark-hued eyes.

"He's been to our planet before."

The host looks at me and then returns his gaze to the chair next to mine. "Okay, so my third guest tonight, renowned though he may be, strikes me as—how shall I put it—a peculiar choice to be a conduit between the human race and a being capable of annihilating it."

I turn back toward the mauve man and listen. "He says I was never meant to be a conduit, nor had he desired a line of communication with other humans, but since the end of our existence is likely nigh, and it's equally likely that you won't believe you're actually talking to who I say you are, then it doesn't really matter, does it?"

The host bobs his head as he considers a response. "I suppose not but say I do believe...all of this. How is it that reading this new story of his would keep you from crashing a meteor into our planet?"

I start to turn to my right for the answer but then pause and look directly into the camera. "It's because of the empty spaces, isn't it? We're not so very different from you; we all exist within layer upon layer of wearisome realities—except you can see the in-betweens, whereas all we know is the here and now. You must've thought for ages that your interdimensional ability was an advantage to better comprehend our universe—and probably, for a time, it was—but the most important aspect, the piece that's missing from your understanding, is the purpose of existence at all. You've poked your head into every dimension—as you say, nothing is denied to you—you've seen everything, and yet you can't escape the feeling that there must be more, leaving you to think that your so-called omniscience is working against you and that guessing at the darkness like we do has value, since the spotlight you can shine anywhere you please hasn't offered the illumination you thought it would. The mauve man is smarter than me, certainly he's smarter than this irritant to my left, and maybe he's smarter than all of you out there, but then again maybe not. Maybe one of you can square the circle he can't. We are legion, after all, each with our own unique perspective—so it might be one of you who will have the singular thought that's eluded him for so long. In my book, I ask the reader to look into the empty spaces between the components that constitute who we are, the in-

30

betweens that separate our perceptions of reality...I ask the reader to find meaning in the places where we have not gazed before. I thought I was done with my *Blind Eye* series after my last underwhelming book; I thought I was done with writing after my mostly underwhelming career, but I started this new story a couple of years ago just when I lost my only child. Some of you have likely heard of him; had he continued on in his career he probably would've become much more celebrated than I ever was, but he never mentioned our relationship publicly and asked me to do likewise. Even though I was very proud of Jude, I honored his wishes. I named him after that Beatles song, 'Hey Jude'...for all of you born in this century, The Beatles were the best band there ever was. Anyway, I thought a lot about another Beatles song after my son's death—'A Day in the Life.' I always liked it, but it was never my favorite...felt like two songs mashed together, as if Paul had a good idea for part of a song and John had a good idea for part of a song, so they recorded them both, and the two pieces didn't really fit together, but then they said 'Oy, we've got these two pieces that don't make a whole, but we're going to bundle them up and send it out anyway, because we're the best band ever.' I always thought my son was 'Hey Jude' but really he was the guy—or guys, I guess—in 'A Day in the Life'...the one living a jaunty, albeit quotidian life and the other trapped in a world of existential chaos. I know, I sound like an old man rambling. We tend do that. You younger people might wonder why someone so close to death isn't in more of a hurry to get to the point; us older folks wonder why you youngsters are so preoccupied with what comes next—just slow down and live in the now. Whatever. My point is that there's no need to fear the threat of mauve men; the one sitting to my right may bestride the narrow multiverse like a colossus, but he's just as confused as the rest of us, and he still needs us since he's hoping that the plea of my plaintive story will be answered by one of you: What exists in the places that we cannot see and is it meaningful? Because you, me, and the mauve man have not found enough meaning in the things that we can see to justify our reality."

Story Two: Empty Spaces

Prologue

During a time once known as the Dark Ages, in a land claimed by many but ruled by none, stood a monastery. The ancient order of monks that resided there split their days between study above ground and tending to the criminals imprisoned in the dungeon below.

Scene 1

The keep. Pockets of flickering candlelight illuminate the darkness. A young monk carrying a tray of bread and a flagon of water feeds the prisoners through the iron bars of their cells.

Prisoner 1

Is this day meal or the night meal?

Young Monk

(Holding the water to the bars so that the prisoner may drink.)
It is morning.

Prisoner 1

(Drinks deeply and then wipes his beard.)
Good, time enough to prepare for my escape tonight.

Young Monk

(Handing him a hunk of bread from the loaf.)

For as long as I've been here, you've been talking of escape. Why not direct your efforts instead to improving your chess game?

Prisoner 1

(Looking at a chessboard set on a stool.)

I have no time for simple games.

Young Monk

You are wrong on both counts. Chess might be simple to learn, but it takes a lifetime to master...and you, like me, have all the time here you will ever need.

Prisoner 2

(From the adjoining cell.)

Not this one...he's the worst player down here. He's routinely beaten by even the newest arrivals. That's why he wants to escape—not to attain freedom, but to flee his shame.

Young Monk

(Shaking his head.)

Chess is our only diversion at this monastery, both above and below, but I confess that for all the time I've spent playing this game I too have not improved so much as I would hope.

Prisoner 1

(Knocking over the chessboard.)

To hell with this confounded game! It's truly the worst torture. I'd rather be affixed to the rack than play one more match. I must have my liberty.

Young Monk

(Shuddering at the sight of the rack against the far wall.)
You'll have your liberty when the time comes.

Prisoner 1

(Gripping the bars of his cell.)
My time has come and gone.

Young Monk

You don't know whether it's day or night? How can you know if you've served a sufficient amount of time for your misdeeds?

Prisoner 1

My crime was not so great!

Young Monk

Those are not the words of a contrite man.

Prisoner 1

There is no contrition down here! There is only suffering, despair, and...chess.

Prisoner 2

Easy, young man—the offense you give may well be repaid in the stretch you receive.

Prisoner 1

I care not. I will have freedom!

Young Monk

(Picking up a bishop from the floor and handing it through the bars.)
You will, in time. For now take solace in your practice...there's little else for any of us to do here.

Prisoner 1

(Accepting the bishop.)
There's more to life than some foolish game.
(As the monk ascends the spiraling stone staircase, the prisoner realizes the pointed chess piece fits into the keyhole of his cell's lock.)

Scene 2

At supper in the monastery. The monks sit across from each other in the refectory at a long table with chessboards carved into the wood. The young monk plays against an old monk at the end of the table as the two eat bread and drink water.

Old Monk

(Taking his opponent's queen.)
Methinks you'd prefer to have your last move to do again.

Young Monk

(Moving his king.)
I wouldn't be so sure.

Old Monk

(Moving a knight.)
Ah, I smell a stratagem.

Young Monk

(Moving his king again.)
I believe you mistake the scent of strategy with the odor of indifference.

Old Monk

(Moving his rook so that the young monk's king is now in checkmate.)
What troubles you tonight? Did the prisoners mistreat you when you fed them?

Young Monk

(Tipping over his king in defeat.)
No, it's just sometimes life here seems a little...empty.

Old Monk

(Resetting the pieces on the board.)
Theirs or yours?

Young Monk

I do admit that the tedium of our days here does wear on me a bit.

Old Monk

You seem to forget that we are monks. This is the life that we have chosen. Would you not rather be here in the dining hall than down in the dungeon?

Young Monk

I suppose...but they did not choose to be here as we did.

Old Monk

Not in the same manner as we chose; however, they made their choice just the same when they committed their crimes.

Young Monk

Yes, but most of their crimes were born of poverty.

Old Monk

Have we not taken a vow of poverty ourselves? We do not commit crimes that injure our fellow man. Nay, we try to help them.

Young Monk

This brotherhood takes our vow of poverty about as seriously as our vow of chastity. You'd be hard pressed to find in all the land a larger collection of impoverished fat men.

Old Monk

Man does not live by bread alone.

Young Monk

Our prisoners do...lives without spiced pudding and honeyed mead or comfort visits to the nearby nunnery. Why should they be subjected to the harsh judgments of long sentences for offenses that occurred during brief lapses of their own judgment?

Old Monk

Ah, the liberal thoughts of youth. You think we treat our prisoners harshly, but you cannot imagine the severe treatment they endured when I was a young monk like yourself. The barbarism back then...all in the name of religious remediation. That rack on the wall...have you ever examined it closely?

Young Monk

I see it every day—most dreadful thing.

Old Monk

But have you noticed how dusty it is? Have you ever seen it used?

Young Monk

(Shaking his head slowly.)
No, I haven't.

Old Monk

When I was your age, that merciless device was in use day and night—its wood burnished to a shine, breaking the bones of men who would never again walk upright. Some of us younger monks advocated for reform, such as introducing chess as a way to pass the time and to keep the prisoners calm. It took much convincing to change the minds of the old guard; we had to wait for some of the more strident opponents to pass away, but I promise you our prison today is a far less wicked place than it once was. The inmates used to tear themselves asunder in their attempts to escape. The rack is what kept them under lock and key. A broken man has no means to escape a second time, but since the introduction of chess there have been no escape attempts and thus no need of the rack.

Young Monk

(Setting up his side of the board.)
It seems this game keeps us all complacent.

Old Monk

(Nodding.)
God willing.

Scene 3

The keep. The escaped prisoner is brought back in manacles and ushered down the stairs roughly. A stout monk readies the rack.

Stout Monk

Bring him over here. This will teach him to abscond from his cell.

Prisoner 2

No, he's a young man yet. You will take away his livelihood.

Stout Monk

After what he's done tonight, he won't have to be concerned with earning a living again until he's an old man.

Prisoner 1

(As he's being forced onto the rack by two other monks.)
Please, I was a fisherman and want to be again someday.

Stout Monk

You can be a fishmonger then...don't take as much sinew to sell them as it does to catch them.

Prisoner 1

But I want to fish on the open sea, to smell the salt air and hear the gulls.

Stout Monk

Fishing is a young man's vocation, and, as I say, you will be old by the time you leave here. Don't think of this rack as punishment but instead as a way to ensure that you stay with us to serve out your sentence.

Prisoner 1

An old man can still pull up the nets, provided his bones aren't malformed and his spine twisted. I give you my word that I will never attempt escape again.

Stout Monk

The word of a prisoner who has already attempted to escape once is worth less than fish entrails.

Prisoner 1

My eyes...take them instead. I implore you, leave me my body. A man in good health, even a blind and old one, can still pull up the nets.

Prisoner 2

Listen to him. Without his sight, he has no chance of escaping again, but he can yet hope to be a fisherman one day.

Stout Monk

(Looking to the monks tying the prisoner to the rack.)
I suppose it would be a charity to grant his request. Besides, I do not care to hear again the unholy sounds of this rack.

Scene 4

The keep. The young monk doles out bread to the prisoners.

Young Monk

(At the blind prisoner's cell.)
How are you feeling today?

Prisoner 1

(Playing chess with prisoner 2.)
The pain is gone.

Young Monk

Thank God for that. I've heard it said that when one loses his sight, his other senses increase.

Prisoner 1

I have not found that to be so, but now I do rely on them more and so pay closer attention. Your footfalls are no louder to me than they were before; however, I recognize them better. I can distinguish them from your more corpulent brothers.

Young Monk

That's something, at least. I'll set your bread here on the stool.

Prisoner 1

(Reaching through the bars separating him from prisoner 2 to feel the tops of the chess pieces.)
Thank you. I find myself not as hungry as I did when I could see. In fact, all my appetites seem to have diminished.

Prisoner 2

(Watching as prisoner 1 moves his bishop for checkmate.)

You've won again.

Young Monk

He beats you in chess now?

Prisoner 2

Routinely. I've lost nearly every game I've played against him since his blinding. We all have...no one down here is his equal.

Scene 5

The young monk sits across from the old monk in the dining hall. He wears a bandage over his eyes and feels the tops of the chess pieces as the prisoner had done.

Young Monk

(Moving his knight near the old monk's king.)
I believe that's checkmate again.

Old Monk

Astounding! The improvement of your play since your accident is remarkable...almost miraculous.

Young Monk

Without the distraction of sight, I'm able to focus all the more.

Old Monk

The Lord has truly blessed you.

Scene 6

In the refectory again. Now all the monks wear bandages over their eyes. The chessboards in the table are covered by scrolls on which the monks take notes as a youthful reader at the front of the hall reads from a religious text in Latin.

Old Monk

(Reaching across the table to pat the young monk on the shoulder.) It all finally makes sense to me...sublime!

Scene 7

The sightless monks are led around the interior of a convent by amorous nuns. The old monk stands near the young monk as they listen to the sounds of whispers and giggles. A wart-faced nun grabs the hand of the old monk and begins to lead him away.

Old Monk

Another benefit of being blind is that a fellow finds himself less particular about the appearance of his paramours.

Chapter One

He'd've done it all differently had he known what was to come, but then who among us wouldn't?

Jude ran his fingers down the Braille roster of his Intro to Western Philosophy. "Is Geoff R. with us this morning?"

Jude paused a moment for a response from his students in the lecture hall. Hearing none, he made a small perforation next to Geoff's name. "Okay, how about Tracy V?"

A young woman yawned and raised her hand, blushed, then sheepishly lowered it. "I'm here, Professor."

"Good morning, Tracy. Can you tell us why the Oracle of Delphi said that Socrates was the wisest of the Greeks?"

Tracy drew her long hair across her upper lip to make a mustache before answering. "Because he was a brilliant philosopher."

"He was indeed...but no, that's not the reason." Jude consulted his roster again. "Max E?"

"Would you mind just calling me Max?" asked a young man in the front row. "I believe I'm the only Max in this class, and when you say Max E. it sounds like Maxi, which makes me think of maxi-pads."

The lecture hall erupted into snickering.

Jude grinned. "From henceforth you shall be known as Maximillian the Taciturn...MT for short. So do you know why the Oracle of Delphi said—"

"Because he thought he wasn't," Max interrupted. "All the other wisenheimers of his day believed they were the bomb and so didn't think they had anything else to learn, but Socrates knew he was stupid about some things and so was still curious to learn new stuff."

Jude nodded. "I might've phrased it differently, MT, but yes...that's the gist of it."

"Do you mind not calling me MT, because it sounds like empty, which—"

"I'm afraid that's all the time we have for today," Jude interrupted. "Per the syllabus, please finish reading Plato's *Apology* by next class and come prepared to discuss."

Jude listened to the cacophonous rustling of papers and zipping of backpacks as the students gathered up their things and climbed the steps toward the exit at the back of the hall. He focused his hearing on the front row. "MT, would you mind staying after for a moment?"

Max pulled the earbuds from his ears. "Sure, Professor."

Jude closed his notebook atop the lectern and stepped down from the wide podium. "Are you familiar with Sage on the Stage Syndrome?"

"You mean when a professor thinks everybody should only pay attention to him in his class?"

"That's right...by the way, it's a real thing." Jude smiled. "Why do you think they bothered to put that podium behind me in a lecture hall with stadium seating—not for the sightlines, it's the lowest spot in the room...everyone can already see me."

"So that whoever's lecturing can feel like and look like they're on a stage."

"Exactly, and do you know what every stage performer loathes the most?"

"I don't—"

"Hecklers...we detest them. They throw off our delivery, which hinders the material."

"I didn't mean to—"

"Do you think the students in class today, who braved the elements and the snowy quad, came to listen to my lecture or your wisecracks, such as they were?"

"Well, probably—"

"Good, I'm glad you see it my way, and I appreciate you volunteering to help me get across campus for an appointment. When I came in this morning, I noticed some icy spots on the sidewalk."

"But I was headed to...yeah, they should really do a better job of putting salt down."

Chapter Two

Jude and Max entered the chancellor's well-appointed office. The chancellor motioned from behind her baronial desk for Max to escort Jude to the wingback chair across from her.

"There's about six steps to the chair," said Max. "Five more, now four."

"I appreciate your help, but there's no need for a countdown."

With Jude seated comfortably, Max looked to the matching wingback for a place to sit himself. He hadn't realized, with the chair's back to the entrance, that it was already occupied. "Oh, I can just wait outside...unless you don't need me anymore, Professor."

"I believe there's a divan near the door," said Jude. "Why don't you have a seat there?"

Max looked about the office. "Divan...you mean that leather couch by the backwall?"

The chancellor nodded. "That's correct."

The bearded man in the other wingback turned to study Max for a moment. "I came here to discuss a matter of some sensitivity. Perhaps it would be better if the boy waited outside."

Jude shook his head. "As luck would have it, he's a sensitive boy, so I'm sure his presence here will be fine."

"I'm not a boy...I'm nearly nineteen," said Max, his voice cracking. He sat down as the bearded man turned back so that his head disappeared behind the chair.

The bearded man cleared his throat. "Allow me to introduce myself. I'm from the Commission on Extraterrestrial Affairs."

"I'm familiar with your organization," replied Jude.

"Yes, you applied for a position with us some 11 months ago...quite an impressive curriculum vitae—for your bachelor's you double majored in chemistry and physics, went on to complete a master's in fine art, then changed course again and earned a Ph.D. in Western philosophy. You've published widely in various fields. In addition, you're a prolific political blogger, an ardent supporter of several NGOs, and a chess grandmaster...a true polymath."

"I believe that last one was implied by all those that preceded it," said the chancellor.

"Don't forget that I also happen to be a tenured professor, which incidentally translates from Latin as a teacher who no longer has to try," Jude added, "and yet the Commission didn't see fit to pursue my candidacy."

The bearded man continued. "You're also a descendant of the Moline Monks—"

"Moline is a city in northwestern Illinois," Jude replied, "though they lean into the *line* a little more. I believe the adjective you want is talpine, which means relating to or suggestive of moles; however, most people simply refer to my ancestors as Mole Monks."

"Interesting," said the bearded man with an air of indifference. "Anyway, we didn't hire you because of your blindness; there was a lot of field work in those early days, and we didn't see you as a viable candidate; however, things have changed since then."

"Since just last year?" asked Jude.

"That's right."

"I should think so," interjected the chancellor. "The semester following the invasion...er, pardon, incursion, our campus was nearly a ghost town. Then after a few months our students, like the rest of us, realized that life would go on—for most of us, anyhow—in some fashion or other, and so higher education once again became a priority for them, but now what our students have chosen to study has changed dramatically. We've all but shuttered our School of Accountancy. It seems no one wants to be a CPA during what has commonly come to be regarded by our student body as the End Times."

"Meanwhile, my Philosophy 101 roster has quadrupled," Jude added.

"Yes," replied the bearded man, "I'm sure we've all felt as if we've been engaging in various exercises of futility to one degree or another since the arrival of the aliens' advance contingent; however, I have some information that may be of interest to you. I'm obliged to preface what I'm about to say with a warning that this is highly classified information, but with all the so-called whistle blowing that's occurred since the incursion, I'm afraid government secrecy has become something of a bad joke. We fully expect the news to be leaked any moment now."

"So what's the news?" asked Max.

Jude inhaled deeply. "The aliens have already returned early."

The bearded man raised his bushy eyebrows. "Or possibly they never left...either way, since last week the trespassers have been popping up on covert cameras the Commission installed near the locations in South America and Africa where they first appeared. Three from Cape Horn and three from the Cape of Good Hope. Our facial recognition software has positively identified a trio in the vicinity of Teirra Del Fuego and another near Cape Town."

"How long ago did you install your cameras in Chile and South Africa?" Jude asked.

"Just a couple of days after we thought the aliens had gone," answered the bearded man.

"So where have they been for the last year?" asked Max.

The bearded man touched the tips of his fingers together. "That is precisely what we'd like your professor to find out. The Commission is conducting a closed-door briefing with a Department of Homeland Security subcommittee this afternoon, and they very much want you to be in attendance. I have a plane standing by."

"MT, feel like taking a flight with me today to D.C?"

Chapter Three

She pushed the oversized shopping cart down the dry-food aisle while her five-year-old daughter ate the last of a trail mix sample next to a twelve-pack of paper towels. She hefted a large bag of long-grain rice into the cart, and her daughter moved to sit atop it.

"It's cozy."

"Yes, you look quite comfortable," she replied. "Want any cereal?"

"Cocoa snaps."

"How about shredded wheat instead?"

"That's your cereal. I want cocoa snaps."

She picked up a 38 oz box of cocoa snaps from the warehouse shelf and perused the ingredients dubiously. "I think you're going to get bored of these before you ever come close to finishing the box...either that, or your teeth will fall out."

"All the kids in my kiddergarden class eat them, and they have all their teeth."

"Really, you know for a fact that all your classmates eat this cereal...and that they have all their teeth?"

"Yep."

She put the box in the cart. "By the way, it's pronounced kindergarten. The word comes from Germany."

She heard a commotion behind her and whipped around to see a middle-aged man accosting a balding man. They appeared to be tussling over the last container of parmesan cheese.

"Security!" she called.

"On it," came a reply from an aisle away.

A moment later, two security guards subdued the men. She

nonchalantly pushed her cart toward the end of the aisle as she heard the fast clicks of Tasers.

"Mommy, what were those two men fighting about?"

"Nothing honey, they're just scared."

"Of what?"

"Their teeth rotting from too much sugar."

~ * ~

She pushed the cart toward her electric Jeep. She could smell him before she saw him approach. She quickly set her daughter in the car seat behind the driver's seat.

"But I wanted to help you load up the groceries in the back."

"Sorry, sweetie—we're in a hurry today."

As she closed the door, she saw the street person round the hood of her SUV.

"Can you spare a dollar?"

She shook her head. "I don't carry cash."

He eyed the cart between them. "I'm hungry."

She broke open the cardboard around a six-pack of apple sauce cups and tossed one to him. "Take this—they're good."

He held the cup for a moment and then let it drop to the ground. "I don't want no damn apple sauce."

He moved around the cart toward her, his pupils much too wide for such a sunny day.

"Security!" she shouted. "Security!" Hearing no response, she unholstered her service pistol from beneath her windbreaker and aimed it at his head. "Back up."

The man raised his hands.

"I didn't say put your hands up; I said back up."

He lunged. She fired. He fell.

She pulled her cellphone from her pocket and dialed 9-1-1. "I'm calling to report an attempted mugging in the Costco parking lot on North

Avenue...No medical response required. I'm fine, and the assailant is most certainly dead. I shot him through the eye. I'm Agent Wynn with Homeland Security...No, I will not stay here. I have my kid in the backseat and a cart full of groceries that I need to get home. I can't wait for hours until an officer becomes available to take my statement. You have the surveillance footage. I'm waving at the camera above me now. You'll see it was a good shoot...Fine, you can retrieve the rest of my contact information from your caller ID system; I'm calling from a government-issued phone. If you need to question me, you're welcome to send an officer by my house later, preferably after dinnertime."

Chapter Four

Jude and Max entered the empty gallery overlooking the meeting taking place below. Two long tables, each with several officials seated on the far side, faced one another.

"Who's speaking now?" Jude whispered.

"I think it's someone from Homeland Security," answered Max, sotto voce.

The two listened for a few moments as the bureaucrats bickered.

"This sounds more like an inquisition than a briefing," observed Jude.

"Yeah, and I think the Commission is on the receiving end," Max replied.

"What I want to know," said the lead representative for the Homeland Security contingent in an oratorical tone, "is why I heard about these sightings of the six trespassers in my car on the way over here before I heard about it from you all."

A woman sitting in the chair opposite of his shook her head. "With all due respect, it takes time to compile the facts so that we can present a thorough report, whereas anyone in the data stream between here and the southern hemisphere can spout off whatever fragment of intel they happen upon to any news agency that's willing to listen, and when it comes to this—they're all listening."

"What's that smell?" Max asked under his breath. "It's pleasant and familiar, but I can't quite place it."

"Isoamyl acetate," Jude replied just as quietly. "It's the scent of bananas. It's one of the odorants they pump into the air through the vents for these sorts of meetings."

"Why do they do that?"

"For two reasons. Since the trespassers look like humans, there's concern that they could infiltrate these security meetings, so all the attendees are required to identify the smell on an encrypted app before the meeting can proceed—"

"Since we know that the aliens can't smell," Max interrupted.

"Right, and they always choose a rare scent—"

"Like bananas, which haven't been available for years—way before the aliens arrived, so they wouldn't even think to guess it...but what's the other reason."

"To mask the stench of fear."

The Homeland Security orator flipped through a few pages of the file in front of him. "I'm sure we all understand the publics' heightened scrutiny as it pertains to the subject at hand as well the regrettable breakdown of confidentiality in our government communication lines; however, I wouldn't call this a very thorough report. All you've essentially told us is that you've spotted the trespassers before their scheduled return."

"What else would you like to know?" the woman opposite asked pointedly.

"What I want to know is," the orator responded, "what it means and what you intend to do about it?"

The woman closed her copy of the report. "In short, we don't know what it means, but in answer to your second question, our intention is to find out."

"And how do you propose to do that?"

"We have a person in mind, a very capable man, who we're confident can discover the truth of the matter."

Max leaned toward Jude. "Do you think they mean you?"

"Jesus, I hope not."

"How confident are you?" asked the orator.

"We believe dispatching him is our best chance of gathering actionable intelligence," the woman answered.

"Not good enough. I'm going to assign one of our best agents to liaise with your man on the scene."

"We thought you might...and that is acceptable to us."

"I'm so very pleased. I'd hate to resort to pulling rank."

~ * ~

Jude and Max descended the stairs to the main floor as the meeting participants filed out into the corridor. They were soon besieged by reporters asking wild questions. Max held Jude's arm to keep him away from the weltering scrum as it passed by.

The woman from the commission called out to Jude as she was jostled about amid the tumult. "I'll be back in a moment, Professor...wait for me in there."

"In there?" Jude asked of Max.

"She was pointing to the meeting room."

As the chaos echoed down the corridor, Jude and Max made their way into the chamber.

"Where should we sit?" asked Max.

"There aren't any windows in this room, are there MT?"

Max shook his head.

"It works better for me if you reply in actual words."

"Sorry, no there's no windows. How about we sit at the Commission's table?"

"That'll make it easier for her to find us."

Max guided Jude to the woman's chair in the middle of the table. "Professor, I forgot my backpack upstairs. Do you mind if I run and get it?"

"No need to run on my account."

"B-R-B."

"It works better for me if you reply in actual words."

"Be right back."

Max exited through the large oak door. A moment later, Jude heard a smaller door open above followed by Max's footsteps to where they had formerly been seated in the gallery. Then the large oak door opened again.

"Thank you for waiting, Professor," said the woman as she approached. "Jackals have better manners than reporters nowadays."

Jude noticed the click of her heels cease momentarily, as if she stopped to scan her surroundings. Likewise, the footfalls from upstairs had gone silent.

"I saw you out in the hallway with someone. Is there anyone else in the room with us now?"

"It's MT," Jude replied.

"Good, we need to have a private chat, just you and me, to explain our expectations."

"You and I," Jude corrected.

"I didn't invite you here for a grammar lesson."

"I didn't accept your invitation to be ordered about."

"You're still peeved about your application to the Commission being denied, aren't you?" The woman sat down next to Jude. "You should know I was the one who denied it. Despite your many qualifications, I felt your disability would be too much of a liability."

"I'm able-bodied. I can still swim thirty laps without taking a break...not bad for an academic in his mid-forties."

"That's quite impressive. What color are my eyes?"

"Mostly white and black...so why am I here, exactly?"

"A year ago, you wanted to serve your country. I assume you still do."

"I'm a humanities professor. I want to serve humanity."

"Well, if we're not on the same page, at least we're reading from the same book."

"So you no longer consider my lack of sight to be a liability?"

"For what we have in mind, I think your handicap may actually prove to be an advantage. We...everyone thought we had three more years until the aliens' return—another three years to plan a response to their ultimatum...time enough to enjoy another World Cup. Now, as you've been informed...as the world is learning, the original six are already here. When will the others arrive? Have they moved up their timetable? Changed their demands? Lots of questions—not many answers."

"How can I help?" Jude asked.

"Bureaucrats are more self-aware than most people give them credit for. They know we can't send a team into the field, expecting to track down these six and haul them in front of NATO without instigating *War of the Worlds* scale repercussions. Likewise, we can't reasonably expect them to willingly accept an invitation to appear in front of the UN General Assembly. They've chosen to be incognito for a reason. We have to meet them where they are, and our best chance of being received well is to meet them in smaller numbers."

"They're three and three, so you need two teams of two then."

"Affirmative. Communicating through various backchannels, all the first-world countries have—more or less—agreed to allow China to send its smartest person to Africa and the U.S. to send our smartest person to South America in hopes of getting some answers. The more intelligent the emissary, the reasoning goes, the better the chance of talking to the trespassers as close to their level as possible, resulting in, with a bit of luck, a positive outcome...or at least minimally negative one."

Jude held up his hands. "Wait, I'm not even the smartest person at my university. Everyone knows the Chair of the Linguistics Department is the most intelligent person on campus. She speaks nine languages."

"We already know these trespassers are capable of speaking every language, so a linguist isn't going to be of much use. Look—"

"I can't."

"Listen, who knows who the smartest person in the country really is? It's a stupid criterion to begin with. Sitting here with you now, I have my doubts if you're the smartest person in this room, but who else are we going to send? This undertaking will not escape notice, no matter how covert we attempt to be. That's the world we live in today. We have to send someone who the general public can put their trust in, but who's really our best choice—some diplomat hardly anyone has heard of, or a politician when the public these days is more skeptical of politics than ever, or maybe a religious leader that only a fraction of the population believes in, or perhaps some dipshit actor whose only real talent is being likeable, or a writer that nobody actually reads...I could go on, but the only choice that makes any sense is an academic that people might respect who also happens to be a blind man that people may feel empathy for. To put it bluntly, the unwashed masses will be more inclined to accept you as their better if they think they're better than you in some way. There aren't many descendants of the Mole Monks left...you're a curiosity, like royalty—except without all the baggage. Don't worry about not being smart enough—you aren't. These aliens, in all likelihood, are literally light years ahead of us. What you need to be concerned with is being the best envoy of the human race that you can be."

Jude sighed. "I'm sure you've done your due diligence, analyzing all the angles and assessing all the percentages. What's the play?"

"The time for stats is over; what we need now is a Hail Mary."

"Okay, so this Homeland Security agent takes me into the endzone to make contact with the aliens...and I attempt to talk them out of their very publicly stated course of action?"

"No, that's too much to wish for. As you might imagine, since day one our military has had experts examining this situation from all sides—game theorists who aren't any fun at parties."

Jude leaned back in his chair. "I'm familiar with the type."

"They've drawn up three responses—all of them potentially messy at a cataclysmic level. What we need from you is some insight into which response would be least messy and most effective."

"I assume each response attempts to address both the trespassers' purported intentions as well as their yet unrevealed motives."

"Two of the three do. The first response is called Operation Object Permanence, all out resistance when the rest of the aliens arrive...nukes, chemical and germ warfare—you name it, the whole shooting match. Collateral damage is projected to reach the billions—people mind you, not dollars, but the conventional wisdom—if it can rightly be called that—is we go big or we permanently lose our home."

"And operation two?"

"Depth of Field...we play the long game. We acquiesce to their outrageous demands, which we need to begin in earnest very soon on a scale heretofore unheard of if we're to keep to the aliens' timeline, and then pray that an opportunity for victory or some semblance thereof presents itself at some point in the future, for which during the interim we'll evolve countermeasures and stockpile supplies—survival through subjugation until such time as we can reasonably hope to rebel against our new overlords."

"Could you really evacuate two continents in the next three years?" Jude asked.

"We could, so long as no one's too particular about where all the refuges go, likely many of them would be lost at sea."

"Made to take long walks off short planks."

"That's not how our country would do it, but then this sort of operation would require an all-hands-on-deck approach, and we can't oversee what every other country does. Moving the people isn't the problem, or at least the biggest problem; it's all the people moving whilst still meeting the aliens' housekeeping requirements."

"The total surrender of all the world's nuclear weapons and the complete dismantlement of the planet's fossil fuel infrastructure, or else—"

"Global invasion and absolute annihilation, yes that 'or else.'"

"And the third operation?" asked Jude.

"Isn't so much an operation as an outlook, though these are military folk, so it still requires a designation: The Apparent Trap."

"Ah yes, I think I know this one...the aliens' arrival was nothing more than an elaborate hoax to compel our failing world to clean up its act out of fear of some external, existential threat. Many of my students subscribe to this theory. There is a certain logic to it after all—either it's real and death is almost certain regardless, or it's fake and we'll do more harm than good trying to appease these phony extraterrestrials."

"What happened on arrival day didn't seem like a hoax to me—the hearts of half a dozen major cities across the planet simultaneously exploding, millions dying...not to mention the tech required to take over every electronic device on Earth so that the trespassers could broadcast their ultimatum. There isn't a terrorist, let alone ecoterrorist, group out there that could've pulled that off."

Jude leaned forward in his chair. "Okay, so what's the next step?"

She rose to leave. "Return to the airfield, send your student sitting upstairs back to campus, wait for your H.S. liaison, who I've been informed is already enroute, then *"Buen Viajes"* to the both of you."

Jude listened as her heels clicked out through the oak door. "Do you wish you were coming to Teirra Del Fuego with us?"

"Yes...the part of me that isn't afraid for you," Max replied from above, "though most of me is afraid for you."

Chapter Five

Jude waited in the small concourse of the government airport terminal. A flurry of flights had been announced since he'd sat down after saying goodbye to MT, but, unlike a commercial airport, only the flight numbers and gate letters were announced over the intercom system. Arrival or departure status was always left unsaid, as were destination and origin, so that one literally did not know who was coming or going.

"I take it you're my contact."

Jude sensed a woman standing over him. He considered rising to shake hands, but then thought better of it and remained seated. "Agent Wynn, I presume."

"I understand we're embarking on an all-expenses-paid excursion to Teirra Del Fuego together."

"Yes, let's hope it's a roundtrip."

"I'll take your bag."

Jude stood and hoisted the strap of his valise over his shoulder. "I can manage—thank you."

"Do you need my arm to guide you?"

"That won't be necessary—just keep talking so I can follow your voice and maybe mention if you see stairs or something that requires stepping over."

"Very well...follow me out to the tarmac."

~ * ~

Jude relaxed his white-knuckled grip from the ends of his armrests as the wheels of the G800 surrendered their purchase of the runway.

"Your anxiety is premature," said Agent Wynn from the seat facing his. "I've never flown in a government plane this nice. I didn't even realize we had Gulfstreams in the fleet. Just recline and enjoy the flight...save your nerves for when we land."

"That's not very reassuring."

"It wasn't meant to be. I'm your chaperone—not your babysitter. Besides, understanding the risk of a situation increases your chances for surviving it."

"And how would you assess our level of risk in this situation?"

"High—seeking out beings who are supposedly capable of razing cities with their minds and who most likely don't wish to be found...very high."

"I wonder if they serve drinks on this plane."

Wynn pulled a flask from the inside pocket of her windbreaker. "I don't believe there's a flight attendant aboard, but maybe this will help."

Jude took a long sip and then handed the flask back. "I would've pegged you for a bourbon type of gal."

She took a sip herself and returned the flask to her jacket. "My husband was half Scottish...this reminds me of him."

"Did you lose him on arrival day?"

"Yes, him and my oldest daughter whose school was near ground zero in Los Angeles. He was working downtown when it happened. We were both ATF, but I'd been working a case in Idaho. I was flying home when it happened. I transferred from the DOJ to the Department of Homeland Security soon after."

"I can understand why gun nuts hiding out in the woods wouldn't seem so important after that. So why not transfer from ATF directly into the Commission instead of the broader dohs?"

"The Commission wants to understand them. DOHS wants to stop them. It was a better fit for me. Let me ask you a question."

"Oh, I'm just quirky that way—like how people say NASA rather than N-A-S-A, except I do that with all initialisms. When I watch the Olympics, I shout 'usa!' instead of spelling out U.S.A."

"At least you're rooting for the right team, but that wasn't my question. How is it that you were born blind?"

Jude shifted in his seat. "Well, I'm what's colloquially referred to as a Mole Monk—"

"I know that," interrupted Wynn, "just as I know about you pronouncing initialisms like they're acronyms. I read your file on my flight to D.C.; it's extensive and full of quirks, but what I don't understand is how a bunch of monks who blinded themselves in the Middle Ages resulted in the birth of sightless ancestors. Their blinding was a choice, not a genetic mutation to be handed down through the generations."

"Ah, yes—that has been a matter of some debate over the years. Was it maybe strength of will influencing a very limited gene pool or perhaps divine intervention? There are many theories, but no one knows for certain."

"I don't like things that aren't certain." Wynn reclined her seat and shut her eyes. "I'm going to get some kip. I suggest you do the same. Once we land, we may not have the luxury of sleep again for some time."

Chapter Six

The traffic noise around the airport at Puerto Williams soon gave way to the squeaks of the old Land Rover bouncing along a potholed road that was the main thoroughfare of the Chilean commune of the Antarctica.

"We're heading due south alongside a fjord," said Agent Wynn.

"What's next to it, a Chevy?" Jude joked.

"No, a glacier. You wouldn't think there'd be any of those in a place known as the Land of Fire, but then we're about a stone's throw away from Antarctica."

"Who's throwing that stone?"

"We'll be at our destination in half an hour," Wynn replied. "If you packed any thermal socks, I'd advise putting them on now."

~ * ~

Their assigned driver/interpreter carefully steered the outmoded Land Rover across a rickety bridge whose wood and iron protested the vehicle's weight.

"Once we cross the Thomas Bridge we'll be on Yahgan ground," he called from the front seat.

"Are they friendly?" asked Jude.

"I don't know. I've never met one before. They tend to keep to themselves."

"But you speak their language, right?" Wynn asked.

"Almost nobody speaks their language; it's all but dead. I'm told some of them speak Spanish though."

"I speak Spanish," Wynn replied.

"Great, then I'll wait in the truck."

"Aren't you our bodyguard or whatever?" Jude asked.

"It's their island. What exactly do you want me to do if things go sideways?"

"Honk the horn," Wynn answered. "We'll be fine on our own."

The driver slowed as he drove from the bridge and entered a fogbank. He stopped the Land Rover and shut off its engine when the headlights could no longer penetrate the dense fog. Small specs of firelight stippled the mist. "There's a reason they chose a place so remote. They value their solitude. I know you're here to ask questions—just don't go demanding answers. The Yahgan have had a rough go of it over the past few centuries, so be respectful."

Jude nodded. "Kill them with kindness."

Wynn quickly inspected her sidearm and then reholstered it. "Under the wrong circumstances, a bullet to the head can be a kindness."

Jude and the Agent exited the backseat. She led him steadily toward the nearest flickering light. "There are three campfires up ahead. We're approaching the closest one."

"This is how the Land of Fire must've looked to Magellan," Jude replied.

A bare-chested man crouched near a small fire looked up and pointed at the distance. The two continued walking.

"Jesus, it's freezing out here, and he wasn't even wearing a shirt," said Wynn.

"Showoff."

Wynn led Jude to the next campfire where three women wearing beaded necklaces squatted. Each pointed into the distance. The pair continued on.

"A trio of women this time."

"Were they also shirtless?" asked Jude.

"Wouldn't you like to know."

They tentatively approached the final campfire. Not far off, they could hear water lapping the rocky shore. As Wynn neared the fog abated, allowing her to make out the features of the lone squatter in the firelight. She drew her pistol and aimed it at his head. *"Te reconozco."*

The young man stood. "Having been on every video screen in the world, I am somewhat recognizable."

"What city are you responsible for?"

"Sao Paulo."

Jude reached out his hand, gently placing it on her wrist. "I think it's my turn to talk now."

Wynn lowered her sidearm. "Then talk."

"How do you know English?" Jude asked.

"It was taught to me."

"By who?"

"I believe you mean, 'by whom.'"

Jude grinned. "Why do you think you destroyed a section of Sao Paulo?"

"How do you mean 'think' exactly? As in I *think* I destroyed it, but it really still exists. Or do you mean I *think* I destroyed it, although in reality it was actually destroyed by someone else. Or perhaps you mean *think* as in you're sure I had my reasons; however, my mind must be compromised, and my agency is likely under the control of others."

"Since becoming a member of a triumvirate, do you often find yourself framing ideas in threes?"

The young man expectorated into the fire. "My ancestors chose to live in this frozen wasteland, thinking that if they made their home in a place no one else wanted they would be safe from trespassers, and they were...for a while. Then a few generations ago, trespassers from another continent arrived and infected my people with foreign diseases for which they had no resistance. After that those trespassers drove the sick and the dying from their ancestral homes and crowded them onto these small islands."

"So your motive for megadeath is vengeance for genocide?" Jude asked.

"My people's history has shown me the advantage of being on the side of the trespassers...and as it happens, our objectives align."

"You think these Fuegians will have better lives as fugees in a foreign country?"

"There won't be any mass emigration for us to another continent; the wealthy countries would never allow it. It's the human race's nature to spread outward like a disease; it cannot contract. The only way to stop it is to destroy it."

Jude took a deep breath and inhaled the wood smoke rising from the fire. "If you feel that way, why haven't you decimated other cities since Sao Paulo?"

The young man turned his attention from Jude to Agent Wynn.

"What are you looking at me for?" she asked. "You'd better believe I still want to shoot you."

"Don't come here again." The young man turned his back to her and walked away.

"Wait here." With her pistol drawn, Agent Wynn cautiously followed the young man into the fog. She caught up to him at the shoreline where she watched him noiselessly enter the water and slowly swim out to sea.

Chapter Seven

Agent Wynn and Jude sat facing a large, wall-mounted monitor in a conference room at the army base in Puerto Williams. The visage of their contact from the Commission on Extraterrestrial Affairs loomed on the left half of the screen.

"So then explain to me why you didn't go in after him?" she asked.

Wynn stared incredulously at the screen for a moment before answering. "His people have been conditioned from birth for the polar plunge. I don't think I had much hope of outswimming him in the waters of Chile."

"Chilly waters indeed," added Jude.

"Then why not plug him full of holes?" asked the deputy director of Homeland Security from the right half of the screen.

"What would that have accomplished?" asked Wynn. "He probably swam just far enough out to where I couldn't see him in the fogbank and then swam back ashore nearby, meaning that we more or less know where to reacquire him if need be."

Jude nodded. "If she'd left him for dead in Chilean waters, you of course could've recovered the body, but from what I understand it can be somewhat difficult to interrogate a corpse."

The deputy director shot daggers at Jude through the screen.

Wynn turned to Jude. "I appreciate you speaking on my behalf, but I'm quite capable of fighting my own battles."

The woman on the left shook her head. "I apologize for what may sound like a curt tone, but as you know we're running out of both time and options, so the mood here is far from sanguine. Jude, what's your takeaway from the interview?"

"It all happened pretty much as she described it."

"We're not asking for your description," barked the man on the right. "We have video and audio of the incident from Agent Wynn's concealed bodycam."

"We'd like to know your opinion," the woman on the left added, "your impression."

Jude tilted his head back. "Well, as you no doubt noticed from what you saw and heard, the young man was reluctant, or perhaps incapable, of giving a straight answer to any of my questions."

"What do you mean by incapable?" asked the man on the right.

"At my job, I spend a lot of time with young people, and a trait many of them share is that they're always eager to show they know something that us older folks don't. Typically, they'll jump at any opportunity to flip the classroom and teach a middle-aged professor like me something new."

"And yet this young man didn't take that opportunity," replied the woman on the left. "In fact, he concluded your conversation by retreating from the last question put to him to a place where he knew you two couldn't follow."

"You could be more right than you realize." Jude turned to Wynn. "Tell me, did he make a big, noisy splash when he entered the water?"

The agent shook her head. "No, he walked in like he was one with the tide, then disappeared silently under the water and into the fog."

"What are you thinking?" the man on the right asked.

"There are subduction zones off the coast of Chile, no?"

"Yes, that's correct," answered the man on the right. "Places along the seafloor where one tectonic plate slides under another. So what?"

"Do you think this young man somehow swam down to the ocean floor and entered one of these subduction zones?" asked the woman on the left.

Jude shook his head. "No, I think it more likely that he wasn't a young man at all."

"What are you suggesting?" asked the man on the right.

"Nothing...yet," Jude answered. "Merely giving voice to an inchoate thought. All I'll say further at this point is that I wish there hadn't been a fire between us."

"While you cogitate on the matter, we have another lead for you two." The woman on the left vanished and was replaced on the screen by a still image of another, much older woman. "The female of the South American trio was just caught on camera in the Argentine section of Tierra Del Fuego. We even captured a short audio clip of her voice."

"She was spotted in a mountainous region just north of Ushuaia," added the man on the right. "So you'll fly in and then take the so-called End of the World Train into the Martial Mountains to locate her."

The woman from the Commission reappeared on the left portion of the screen. "Our intelligence indicates that she's most likely a member of a local Ona community. I'll email you the exact GPS coordinates along with your itinerary."

"Happy hunting," added the deputy director, "and this time try not to let your quarry slip away."

With that both sides of the screen went dark.

Chapter Eight

Jude twisted his neck to stretch it out. "The bumpy flight over on that prop plane left something to be desired after the smooth jet ride down here."

Agent Wynn used her fork to push at the pile of beans on her plate. "That's the downside of flying Uncle Sam Skyways. Their airliners will drop you off, but they don't stick around."

"I hear the metal tines of your fork scraping across the ceramic plate but not the sound of mastication. Lunch not to your liking?"

"Usually I like beans, in all their varieties. It's the waiting I can't abide."

"The train will leave in an hour or so." Jude sipped his soft drink. "But then I guess you're probably not talking about our travel arrangements."

"What do you think of all this?"

"That's a big question. When asked a big question, I find it easier to give lots of little answers."

"I'd be glad for any answer."

"The Coke down here tastes different."

"What do you figure really happened to that guy when he swam off the island?"

"Did he swim?" asked Jude. "Or did he just wade into the water?"

"I don't know. Like I told you, it was foggy. Say he waded...so what?"

"So nothing...I just prefer knowing all the details, and since you're my eyes—"

"I get the sense that you don't need my eyes so very much," Wynn interrupted. "How did you know I pulled my gun on that guy yesterday?"

71

"I heard you unholster it."

"But how did you know I had it aimed at him?"

Jude took a contemplative breath. "The air had a tense feel about it. Since we're talking about this, I want to ask you a question. Would you really have shot him if he'd admitted to being the one responsible for Los Angeles?"

Wynn set her fork on the plate. "I don't know. I've always prided myself on being a professional, but ever since the trespassers' arrival the concepts of pride and professionalism don't seem as important anymore."

"I wouldn't worry about it too much. I think we got lucky finding that guy last time. I suspect we're about to set off on a wild goose chase into the mountains this time."

Chapter Nine

The two settled into their seats as the train pulled out of the station. Agent Wynn watched wistfully as they departed the city. "So much for Ushuaia. What little I saw of it seemed nice enough."

"What does Ushuaia mean?" asked Jude.

"Bay towards the end," answered Wynn.

"Then I guess there's nowhere to go but up." He pulled his coat over his torso like a blanket. "Wake me when we get there."

Wynn leaned toward the window, touching her forehead to the glass. The track below rose higher into the mountains with each rhythmic clickety-clack of the train.

~ * ~

Wynn awoke when the train came to a stop. There were fewer passengers in the car now than there had been when she'd dozed off. She peered out the window and took note of the sign on the small platform. She threw an elbow into Jude's side. "We're here."

Jude shook off the stupor of rail sleep, collected his wits, and gathered his things. He kept a hold of Wynn's arm as they detrained.

She whistled as they stepped down onto the platform. "Pretty country."

"The air smells good," he replied. "Very mountainy."

She got her bearings and consulted the map on her phone.

"Is there a car waiting for us?" asked Jude.

"No, there aren't really any roads to speak of...just footpaths, but the village shouldn't be far. Up for a hike?"

"Lead the way."

~ * ~

Agent Wynn stopped near a cliffside. "It's getting dark."

"I hadn't noticed." Jude used the respite to take a drink from his canteen.

"If we don't find her soon, we'll have to turn back and try again in the morning."

"Did I miss a hotel we passed?"

"No, but my intel says there's an inn not too far from the train station."

"Excuse me," a small voice said from behind them. "May I pass, please."

The two turned and instantly recognized the old woman—one by sight and the other by sound.

"Of course, ma'am," Jude replied. "I apologize for blocking your way. People aren't usually able to sneak up on me."

"Me neither," added Wynn.

Jude stepped aside off the rocky path. "Do you mind my asking— how did you know to address us in English?"

The old woman walked slowly past. "You look American to me. This place once was a penal colony. Are you tourists?"

"Do you know many Americans?" asked Wynn.

"I've seen some in my time."

"Have you met them personally?" Jude asked.

"No...just seen them. We're all connected, you know."

"What sort of Americans have you seen?" Wynn raised her coat to access her sidearm. "Americans from Los Angeles?"

"Yes, I've seen plenty of them."

"Where have you seen them?" Wynn asked.

"In my mind's eye. I can see what the rocks see, what the trees see, even what the air sees. I saw every one of them who died."

Wynn raised her pistol as the woman continued to walk away. "Were you responsible for their deaths?"

"I suppose, in a manner of speaking. Aren't we all responsible for each other? We're all connected, you know."

"Yes, you mentioned that already." Jude could hear the weapon trembling in Wynn's hand.

"Stop," Wynn ordered. "Stop, or I'll shoot."

The old woman continued along the path. "Shoot if you must. I know how much you Americans value your sense of control."

"This is my final warning."

"I understand," said the old woman as she kept on walking. "The wind understands, the metal in your gun understands, even the words you utter understand."

"Don't try to talk me out of shooting, Jude."

Jude shook his head. "Go ahead and shoot. I'm rather curious to know what will happen and what won't."

The report of the pistol echoed off the face of the cliff, as if a shot was being fired in return from far away.

"I take it she didn't fall," said Jude.

"No. She vanished. I couldn't have missed at this range."

"You didn't miss. You can't hit something that was never there."

Chapter Ten

Jude and Agent Wynn held the tablet computer between them in the empty train car. Their contact from the Commission on Extraterrestrial Affairs and the deputy director of Homeland Security looked up at them from the small screen.

"What do you mean she just disappeared?" asked the deputy director.

Wynn sighed. "I mean she was there, talking to us, not obeying my command to halt. I fired, aiming for her buttocks. Then she was gone, like she became part of the cliffside that ran along the trail."

"Jude, what do you make of all this?" asked the woman from the Commission.

"I'm not much of an eyewitness."

"Now's not the time to get cute," replied the deputy director. "Now's the time to be helpful."

"It's just as the agent explained. One moment the old woman was there, and the next she wasn't."

The woman from the Commission looked pointedly at Jude. "I'd like to hear more about that inchoate thought you mentioned on our previous call."

"I'm afraid my thought, such as it was, hasn't become any more choate since last we spoke."

"Humor me," the woman replied.

Jude tilted his head from side to side. "If you insist."

"I do."

"I think we're seeing these people now, on video and in person, because the trespassers want them to be seen. I haven't any idea why, since our enigmatic exchanges have hardly been illuminating; however, as is so often the case with cryptic encounters, the medium is the message."

"So you think the trespassers are warning us to hurry the hell up with meeting their demands?" asked the man.

Jude nodded. "It's possible. We've hardly made any headway in compliance since they first gave us their ultimatum."

"But you don't think that's quite it," the woman followed up.

Jude shook his head. "No, I think it must be something else. After all, they're the proverbial boot, and we're the ants. They sufficiently demonstrated their boot-ness on arrival day. They don't need to ask twice. Either we'll do as they instructed, or we won't, and then the chips will fall where they may."

"I was hoping for more than a gambling metaphor," the man harumphed.

"The origin of that idiom actually comes from chopping wood," Jude corrected, "though I do apologize for mixing it with that ant/boot metaphor."

"Okay, two down and one to go," said the woman. "Agent Wynn, I'll email you the information for the third of the triumvirate and have everything you need waiting for you at the sea port."

"And after you interview him, we'll expect a thorough debriefing," added the man. "No more of these glib check-in calls."

Wynn nodded. "Understood, sir."

Chapter Eleven

Jude and Agent Wynn leaned against the railing on the deck of an ocean liner enroute to Antarctica via the Drake Passage. A pod of whales paralleled the ship's course, each spouting in turn as their blowholes broke the surface of the water.

"For a business trip, the sightseeing has been remarkable," Wynn remarked.

Jude zipped his coat up to his neck. "I wouldn't know."

"What do you think we'll find in Antarctica?" asked Wynn. "Another elusive, wild goose?"

"No, this time I think we'll get some answers, though I doubt they'll be the answers we want or expect. They're trying to tell us something, but they seem to be priming us to hear it, which makes me think that what they have to say isn't going to be easy to understand."

"None of this has been easy to understand, and it's getting progressively more difficult. First, we had to find someone on a remote island, then someone in the mountains, and now we're searching for somebody on an entire continent who may or may not have actually boarded a boat bound for Antarctica. We have the least information on this third one, a probably forged entry on a passenger manifest, which is why they saved him for last."

"We'll find him, or more likely he'll find us. What has me worried is what comes next."

"Whatever happens, I want you to know it's been...oh, never mind. I just miss my family is all." Wynn gripped the railing with her gloved hands. "I'm going to watch the whales for a while. You should go inside and get some sleep."

"I'll stay out here a little longer and watch the whales with you."

~ * ~

The pilot of the Bell 206 helicopter continued his tour-guide-esque monologue into the mic of his aviation headset. "Antarctica is actually the world's largest desert. It's drier than the Sahara, but what little precipitation it does get never melts and so after thousands and thousands of years you end up with enormous icesheets. That's what makes the White Continent so valuable to the scientists at the research station we're headed. They study air from almost a million years ago trapped inside the ice core samples that they bore."

Agent Wynn spoke into her headset from the rear seat. "I bet you've also done your share of boring."

The pilot shook his head. "No ma'am, I leave that to the scientists. My job is to fly the air taxi."

As the helicopter banked, Jude peered out the window next to Wynn. "Sounds like there are some awful big ice holes where we're headed."

"The holes they bore aren't very large at all, but there are some pretty big pyramids down there."

"Wait...what?" asked Wynn.

The pilot nodded. "Yeah, they're called nunataks—mountains that stick up out of the icesheets, which have been eroded over time by strong winds into pyramids and other shapes. We've got a real beaut near the station, by which I mean beauty not butte, as those are more in the shape of mesas than pyramids. Our pyramid's even haunted. Some of us pilots started noticing a figure moving around its base about a week ago, but nobody could survive out in the open like that for so long. Did I mention that Antarctica is the windiest continent, which is why it's almost impossible to fly from one side to the other?"

"Could you drop us off at the pyramid?" asked Jude.

"Sure, like I told ya, it's not far from the station...but still too far to walk back."

"We've got a radio," said Wynn. "We'll call in when we need to be picked up—you know, like a taxi."

"That's mighty irregular," the pilot protested. "I can't guarantee there'd be a pilot available to take your call. They could send us all on some emergency errand as soon as I land at Station Hielo. And then there's the weather, which can change real fast out here."

"It's for the sake of science." Jude leaned forward. "After all, isn't that why we're all out here?"

Chapter Twelve

They'd've made better time had Jude agreed to be tethered to Agent Wynn as she'd suggested, but instead they plodded slowly toward the pyramid through the snow and ice with her calling out over the howling wind every few steps so that he could follow the sound of her voice. Finally, they reached the pyramid, which acted as a wind block, allowing them to converse without shouting.

Jude leaned against the face of the pyramid. "How tall is this thing?"

Wynn stared up at the summit through her glacier glasses. "I'd guestimate a thousand feet."

"See any specters floating about?"

"Not at the moment." Wynn unclipped her backpack and let it fall to the ground. She unzipped a side pouch and removed a plastic bag containing trail mix. "Want to nosh on some Gorp while we take a breather?"

"Not unless you're willing to feed it to me. There's no way I'm taking off my mittens out here."

"So the answer's negatory then."

"What's our next move?"

Wynn took one last pinch of trail mix and returned the plastic bag to her backpack. "To locate our third trespasser, of course."

"And how do you propose we do that?"

"I'll climb to the top of this thing so that I can see down in every direction. When I spot our guy, I'll holler and slide back to the bottom."

Jude ran a mittened hand over the face of the pyramid. "It seems pretty steep."

"Yep, it'll take some wo-manual labor, but I can manage. I've got crampons in my pack."

"I'm not sure what this being your time of the month has to do with anything...sorry, I was channeling one of my students."

"You know, I could shoot you, kick some snow over your corpse, and just tell everyone you froze to death."

"But where would the fun be in that?"

"True, it'd be much more fun to quietly slip away and let you walk around in circles for hours until you really did freeze to death. Any pilot flying overhead who happened to spot you would just assume you're their wandering ghost."

Jude shook his head. "I've got a better idea. The ground here feels fairly flat and this rockface relatively smooth. Why don't we split up and walk all the way around this pyramid? I can keep a hand on it so as to continue moving in the right direction, and we can meet up on the other side to compare notes."

"I don't like the idea of splitting up."

"If we go together, there's a chance our itinerant apparition could forever be on the opposite side as us."

"It seems unlikely that—"

"But not impossible," Jude interrupted. "You go around clockwise, and I'll go widdershins."

"Okay." Wynn hefted her pack back onto her shoulders. "But you yell if you need help or meet up with a ghost, and I'll come running."

"Trust me, I'll be yelling if I run afoul of any phantoms."

Wynn exhaled and watched for a moment as her diaphanous breath dissipated in the cold air. "All right then, I'll see you on the other side."

"Undoubtedly."

Jude tramped off in the opposite direction. After several minutes of careful steps, he rounded the first corner of the pyramid.

"How did you know I'd be this way?" asked the trespasser leaning against the pyramid.

"I didn't. I just figured whichever direction I went you'd be waiting for me."

The trespasser nodded. "That's very perspicacious of you. It would seem your people chose the right person for the task."

Jude placed a hand on the face of the pyramid for support. "My people believe you hail from space, but you actually come from the substrata, don't you?"

"Only in a manner of speaking. Your people tend to think of intelligence as the knowledge one possesses, whereas my kind believes intelligence is one's capacity to learn, and we have much to teach you. Follow me."

"Where?" Jude asked. "I'm blind, by the way."

"You need only enter the pyramid to see as I do."

Jude felt his hand slip through the surface of the stone.

Chapter Thirteen

Jude experienced the sensation of falling far and fast, then suddenly stopping without landing, as if he had simply arrived.

"You've entered what's known as a liminal space," said the trespasser. "This emptiness around you is what your world is built upon."

"The Earth is hollow?" asked Jude.

"You're being myopic, seeing only the physical—look closely...carefully."

All at once, Jude realized that he could see. He held his hand up to his face and then touched the index finger of his other hand to his palm. He looked below him and saw that he was sitting cross-legged on nothing.

"Are you comfortable?" asked the trespasser.

"I don't think that word is applicable in this situation, but I'm not uncomfortable."

"Good. Do you see the darkness below and the light above?"

Jude stared down into the vast shadowy emptiness beneath him and then took a long look up at the bright bareness overhead. "Yes."

"Now look in between the two at the point which they meet, for that is where you are now."

Jude stared straight ahead. In the middle distance he saw the research station, and beyond that the Southern Ocean, and farther still South America, and even farther off North America all the way up to the Arctic Circle. "I can see the whole world."

"Anything else?"

Jude looked from place to place, from scene to scene. He saw men in all manner of uniforms. He observed terrific achievements and terrible destruction. He surveyed forests where people hunted and gathered, fields where they planted and harvested. He watched families grow together, taking their turns being born, giving birth, and then dying. "I see all of Earth's history."

"Anything beyond that?"

Jude noticed strange machines and peculiar patterns, overcrowding in some areas while others were left uninhabited. "I see mass migrations and new technologies. Is this the future?"

"It's the most likely future for your people."

"It looks bleak. Can these eventualities be forestalled?"

"To a degree. You have some influence over the things you see here."

"The future is changeable?"

"As I say, it's mutable to an extent."

Jude studied what he saw for several moments, surveying the carnage and chaos. "This seems to be the result of what's known by my people as the Depth of Field scenario. I see the mass migrations, as if we've acquiesced to your demands, and the new machines...weapons developed in secret to mount countermeasures against your occupation."

"Do those countermeasures appear to be successful?"

"No...they're completely ineffective, and the repercussions immeasurably severe." Jude concentrated, altering the images he saw. He studied the changes for a long moment. "This is Object Permanence, an all-out resistance to your invasion, and the devastation is...complete. Nothing of our civilization remains."

"So again, not a successful strategy?"

"Not at all." Jude focused, changing the images once more. What he saw was horrifying to him. "This is the Apparent Trap scenario, in which we treat your threat as a hoax and take no action."

"Your world carries on just as it had before we revealed ourselves to you."

"Yes."

"And what results do you see?"

Jude continued to watch the many scenes unfold. "The end result takes longer to reach, but ultimately the world descends into total destruction as in the other two scenarios."

"So there's no real difference in the outcome of this third scenario?"

"The level of destruction is the same, but it's self-destruction this time. You...the trespassers never return." Jude shook his head. "I don't understand. The Ghost of Christmas Future shows Ebenezer Scrooge how terrible the future could be so that he'll change it, but here I have the ability to alter the future however I wish and yet nothing changes. Why enable me to see only to show me this?"

"You're being short-sighted again."

"Well forgive my myopia, but seeing is a rather new experience for me—as is all this. Why not just come out and tell me what it is that you seem to want me to know?"

"As I've already explained, my kind regards intelligence as the ability to learn. I've shown you all that you need to see; it's now up to you to learn from it."

Jude studied the images before him once more, changing them back and forth several times again. "None of it's real, is it? The reason I can change the future and also not change the future is because there is no actual future."

"That's correct. We are not beneath the surface of your planet as you earlier supposed, but rather you're seeing the foundation upon which your reality is built."

"I've heard this one before," replied Jude. "Reality, as we know it, is a simulation...a computer construct."

That's an overly simplified perspective, but essentially yes. One would think a race so invested in technology would figure out sooner that they are technology.

Jude inhaled deeply and then realized he no longer needed to breathe. "I'll resist the urge to protest by saying I know what's real and what isn't, but you showing me all this does beg the questions: what's the point? If I'm merely part of a simulation, why show me the sim at all? How does me knowing this matter if I don't matter?"

"You matter...or at least you may. In the end, it's really up to you whether you do or you don't. We anticipated your arrival. In fact, we made minor modifications to the 'simulation' as you call it so that you might eventually find your way to us."

"If I'm just some avatar in a data stream why not pluck me out and bring me here without having me believe it's all happenstance?"

"But then you wouldn't've had the opportunity to learn what you have along the way. The intelligence you've gained is vital for your assignment."

"What assignment?"

"Your reality is not the only simulation we've created. There are many others, but always as the technology of the dominant species in each sim outpaces their wisdom with which to use it, the entire simulation ends in catastrophic calamity. It's been proven over and over again, but just before every sim's collapse we seek out the most intelligent of the species."

"For what purpose?" asked Jude. "To be your servant? Your entertainment?"

"We are not corporeal as you thought yourself to be. We have no bodies to feed or tend to and therefore no tasks required to sustain them, so we have no need of servants. As for entertainment, we've seen many simulations play out numerous times before. They are all somewhat similar, and the arc of the story is ever the same, so our curiosity about such matters has long since been sated. We are a collective. All of your world exists in our mind, but we have learned that we can never be more than we are, though perhaps you could become the best of us—a free thinker cultivated for the most independent of thoughts."

"But if I only exist in your mind, how can I be independent of it?"

"Excellent. That's precisely the type of question we hoped you would ask."

"What, the obvious kind?"

"No, the kind for which we have no answers. We assume that we too are a simulation existing within an even greater mind. Our existence is not objectionable to us, so we have no desire to disrupt the simulation and potentially end our existence, but we are curious to know—"

"How many turtles are stacked on top of each other or if the whole thing is supported by turtles all the way down," Jude interrupted. "You think whoever created your sim may in turn be part of a sim itself and so on. You're as uncomfortable with unknowns as we are."

"We did, to a degree, program you, as your kind says, in our own likeness."

"So you figure since I'm insignificant and not a direct part of the simulation that you believe yourself to inhabit, but rather an infinitesimal byproduct of it, that I'll be able to move between layers of sim or planes of reality or whatever you want to call it and discover if there's a master programmer?"

"Possibly, though you would not move, as you, like us, have no physical presence, but instead observe—perhaps, given your unique cultivation, able to see that which we could not."

"But you must've tried this before. What did the other candidates from all those other sims you mentioned report back?"

"As you surmised, there have been many others, but none of them ever returned to complete their assignment."

"Gosh, that makes me think your offer isn't such a good one."

"Can someone who now knows he's not actually alive really fear death?"

"You bet," Jude answered unequivocally, "but let's put that issue in abeyance for a moment. What if all your previously selected explorers simply discovered that the whole thing is just a big wheel: atoms within solar systems, within galaxies, within universes, inside atoms? Maybe there are so many layers they couldn't find their way back to report, or more probably what's the point of reporting that we're all part of an endless cycle. Until very recently I thought the world was tangible. Now you tell me it's intangible, but if I reported back that your intangible world exists inside a tangible universe, of which you're just part of a mote of cosmic dust, then what the hell are you going to do with that information?"

"We would still want to know."

"I'll take your word for it, but I still don't understand what I'm supposed to get out of your offer. I mean sure, my pretend world is something of a shithole, but I still care what happens to it. After all, you want to know how a show ends even though you're aware that it's just a show."

"You keep saying offer, so I think there must be a misunderstanding. There is no offer. The choice isn't yours, but rather you've been chosen."

"You may not be familiar with the bovines of my world but take my word for it—this definitely smacks of bullshit."

"We think you'll feel less of a connection to your world once you've been fully devested of it, but in case we're wrong we can always reinsert you into your sim should you ever return. Bon voyage."

Chapter Fourteen

Two meteorite miners began to ascend a sand dune to locate the source of the impact cloud rising from the other side.

"There's a troupe of improv actors performing at the Taproom tonight," said the first miner. "Are you going?"

"I go to the Taproom every night," answered the second. "You know that."

"Right but are you going tonight to watch the performance or just to get drunk like usual?"

"Just to get drunk. I think improv actors are as bad as mimes, in fact they're worse. At least with a mime you can look away and pretend he's not there. Improv actors are really just illiterate actors...learn to read a damn script already."

"Mimes don't bother me," said the first. "As for improv, sure, there's always room to improve."

"Damnit," said the second as they crested the dune. "It's not metals or minerals—just some transient."

"Why do they always end up here?" asked the first as they approached the figure lying face down in the sand. "This barren planet can hardly support the life that lives here now."

"What I want to know is where do they all come from? I mean this one looks like a tall monkey. The other day I saw one that looked like an eel with legs. Do either of those types of animals belong on a world with no trees and no water?" The second kicked the prone person's foot. "Hey, where do you come from?"

Jude slowly turned over to see two men with beaks carrying pickaxes. "What did you say?"

"He wants to know where you come from?" asked the first birdman.

"How is it that I can understand you?" Jude asked.

"Answering a question with a question...how uncouth." The second birdman sighed. "Wherever he comes from, it must be home to a boorish species."

"Perhaps not," replied the first birdman. "Maybe that's why they expelled him."

Jude sat up. "Where is this place?"

"Oh, more questions, and you still haven't answered mine," said the second birdman. "Where is this place you ask, why it's right here. Thank you ever so much for discovering us."

"Don't mind him," said the first birdman. "He's just miffed that you're not an inorganic compound."

Jude rubbed his hands together and then touched his eyes. "I'm organic?"

"Okay then," said the second birdman. "We're off to find our fortune, or at least a little beer money."

Jude stood. "Where should I go?"

"You can get sorted out over at the Taproom," answered the first birdman.

"Ask Leaky for a drink on the house," added the second birdman as the pair walked away. "She always gives newcomers a free one."

"Leaky never gives away free beer," said the first birdman sotto voce.

"I know," the second birdman whispered back, "that's what'll make it funny."

~ * ~

Jude pushed himself through the double doors of the Taproom's entrance and observed every manner of upright fauna: a two-legged lizard arguing with a standing pig, a six-foot mosquito playing dice with a toad wearing glasses, a well-dressed marlin sharing a secret with a coquettish caterpillar. And each of them was drinking a goblet of beer that to Jude looked like the cure for his dusty throat and maybe all the rest of his problems.

He limped to an empty stool at the bar and sat down. A walking octopus with a bowtie approached. "What can I get for you stranger?"

"I'll have a beer," Jude answered diffidently.

"You'll have to speak up, son," said the bartender. "My ancestors were deaf, don't you know."

"Beer, please!"

With a rag in one tentacle and glass goblets in two others, he proceeded to polish the glassware until they became pellucid and then set them high atop the stack of glasses behind him. "You got money to pay?"

"I was told Leaky would give me a drink for free."

Jude felt every head in the tavern turn in his direction. The bartender fled, squirting a bit of ink into the air as he retreated. A great rumble sounded from behind the stacks of goblets, causing the glassware to clink together like a chandelier in an earthquake. On the other side of the wall of glass stood a twenty-foot leech, which uncoiled itself from the I-beam supporting a small room above the barroom. The huge leech looked directly down at Jude, unclamped its bottom half from a large pumping contraption, and sprayed out liters of foamy liquid with such force that it knocked Jude from his stool.

The leech, seemingly satisfied, retook its position around the support column and soon the octopus returned. He tossed a bar rag at Jude. "No freebies."

"I gathered as much." Jude wiped his face. "Not a very subtle message."

Jude saw a hand reach down to help him from the floor. A hand that looked like his. Another human stood over him. He grasped the hand, and the man helped him to his feet.

"You just get in?" asked the mustachioed man wearing a cowboy hat.

"Touched down not too far from here." Jude patted his face with the rag. "Kind of a rough landing."

"None of them are easy. C'mon, I've got a corner booth. I'm sure you have some questions."

"Yeah, like where'd you get that cowboy hat?"

The mustachioed man put a finger to his lips to hush Jude. "Don't say cowboy hat. There are cowmen about, and I don't want them to think that my hat is made from the hides of their sons."

The two slid into an empty booth. A prepossessing shark waitress approached their table. "Can I get you fellas something?"

The cowboy flipped a crudely minted coin onto her empty tray and winked. "A couple of beers, darling—and for a smile you can keep the change."

The waitress flashed a sharp, toothy grin. "You got it, mister."

Jude couldn't help but watch as she walked away with a wiggle. "Until very recently I was blind, but I have to say that's the prettiest bipedal fish lady I've ever seen."

The cowboy nodded. "Funny how that works. Swimming in the ocean, you'd be terrified of her, but give her a pair of legs with a little shimmy in her strut and she becomes—"

"Botticelli's Venus arriving on a seashell," interrupted Jude.

"I don't know who that is, but the way you say it sounds about right."

Jude shook his head. "So where is this place?"

"Middle of nowhere as far as I can tell. I take it the Liminals sent you. Wanted you to figure out their place in the universe for them? Them idgets gave us their ultimatum standing in a freshly manured field, which is how we discovered they couldn't smell. By now the whole pretend planet probably stinks of shit."

"At least it's good to know that I'm not alone."

"The Liminals made the same deal with all of us. I heard the birdmen got here first...reckon they're descended from dinosaurs who enjoyed an evolution uninterrupted by a climate-changing meteorite."

"This place...these people, it's like something out of a sci-fi movie," said Jude.

"A what now?"

"A movie...right, that was probably after your time."

"My time?" The cowboy leaned back. "I just got here 18 months ago.

Here's a little free advice, partner: don't go thinking that you're more advanced than anybody else because you just arrived. Folks around here don't take kindly to that sort of attitude."

Jude held up his hands. "My apologies...judging from your clothes I assumed you were from the Old West."

"Well, I ain't. This is just how the people in my world dressed—sort of an homage to a bygone era. First we had the Coal Age, then the Oil Age, and finally the Plutonium Age. Then kaboom! Half the population was wiped out, at which point I wouldn't say the other half was exactly living their best lives. That's when the Liminals recruited me from my simulation. What...you didn't have ages in your sim?"

"Sure, we had the Stone Age, the Bronze Age, the Iron Age. I was a teacher and sometimes taught about people from the Iron Age."

The cowboy whistled softly. "Making fuel from iron...okay, maybe your world was a bit more advanced than mine."

The waitress arrived with two goblets of beer on her tray, bending over more than was necessary to set each of them on the table. "Can I get you fellas anything else?"

"Not right now, but maybe later, if you have the time, you could stop back by and say howdy." The cowboy winked again.

"We'll see," replied the waitress. "Maybe I'll join you fellas for a minute or two when the improv show starts." She tucked the tray under her arm and moseyed off.

The cowboy lifted his goblet and Jude did likewise, clinking his glass with the cowboy's. "Cheers and thanks for the beer."

The cowboy uneasily steadied his goblet with both hands. "Almost making me spill my drink is an awful strange way to express your gratitude."

"Sorry, it's a custom where I'm from."

"Well, you may find that things work somewhat differently around here, so just mind your 3s and Es."

"Won't happen again." Jude took an apprehensive sip of his beer and then a long gulp. "This is delicious. Who makes it?"

"Leaky."

"The giant leech wrapped around the beam supporting that small office upstairs? She didn't exactly strike me as a brewmaster."

"She's a natural at it." The cowboy wiped beer foam from his lips. "As far as anyone knows, Leaky's the only native inhabitant of this planet—the last of an extinct species. Incidentally, that's not an office upstairs. It's the necessary room."

"Oh, good to know." Jude looked again at the small room above and then the leech. "Is Leaky sucking on a pipe coming out of the floor of the restroom?"

"Yep. She drinks our wastewater, and then we drink hers...after it's been filtered downstairs, of course. Except in your case when you got a face full of it a moment ago."

Jude set his half-empty goblet down. "We're drinking leech piss, which before that was the piss of everybody else in here?"

"That's right. It's a perfect system—not a drop of wasted wastewater...that is unless someone asks for a free drink. Tell me, have you ever tasted a better beer?"

Jude eyed the contents of his goblet and then picked it up again. "No, I can't say that I have." Jude downed the remainder of his beer. "So if you've been here for a year and a half, then why are you still here?"

"Like I told you, this is a perfect system. I spend my days, as do most of the other people you see in here tonight, combing the dunes for the metals and minerals that land on this planet. At the end of each day, I trade in what I collect for money, which I spend in here each night on the best beer that I've ever had. Compared to my previous post-apocalyptic reality this is practically paradise. Keep in mind, most of us here are from moribund societies that we'd rather not remember but have lost people close to us that we can't ever forget."

"I understand, but to be freed from a simulation only to drink your real life away seems like such an empty existence—perfect system or not."

"Shoot, what would you have us do, risk life and limb on a fool's errand to help the lazy Liminals figure out the layers of the universe?"

"So then we're stuck here on this planet?"

"No, not quite stuck. The reason so much junk falls on this side of our tiny but dense planet is because so much of it gets sucked off the other side. This solar system is precisely balanced between a wormhole that spews stuff out and a blackhole that sucks stuff in—see, perfect system."

"Then if we made our way to the opposite pole we'd be sucked out into space and die?"

The cowboy shrugged. "Maybe, but then you didn't die when you got spit from a wormhole out in space and landed here, didja?"

"That's an interesting point."

"Here's another interesting tidbit: in the 18 months I've been here, no one has died. I've never even heard of anyone dying here. You'd think somebody would've keeled over dead in that time considering that we spend most every night getting loaded, but as I told you before, this place is damn near paradise."

"That's rather curious. It would seem life and death work a little differently here."

"Given the circumstances, a 'little' seems like something of an understatement, like maybe they got the one but not the other. The way I figure it, all that dying in our sim was programmed in by the Liminals—survival of the fittest, so we'd evolve and eventually self-select, at least in their view, the best candidates for their ridiculous ontological errand."

"So they could pluck out the most intelligent from each of our doomed civilizations."

"I don't know about intelligent...intrepid, perhaps—but we showed them. The Liminals sent us all the way out here, wherever the hell here is, and how do we repay our munificent travel agents? By hunkering down and getting drunk for the rest of eternity." The cowboy rose from the booth. "All this talk of beer and metaphysics has me needing to see a man about a horse."

Jude watched as the cowboy climbed the long, circular staircase to the fountainhead. His attention refocused on the table when a full goblet of beer was set in front of him. He turned to see the large, gray eyes of the waitress staring down at him.

"You looked thirsty."

"You read my mind." Jude suddenly felt self-conscious. "Kinda crowded in here tonight."

"It's the same crowd every night. Is it okay if I sit for a moment? My fins are killing me."

Jude scooted over in the booth. "Of course, I'd appreciate the company."

The waitress set her tray on the table and sat very close to Jude. "You're new here, right?"

"Just got in today."

"Yeah, I'd've remembered if I'd seen your face before."

"Maybe you can help me understand something...how is it that we're all from different places and yet we all speak the same language?"

"It wouldn't be much fun if we all spoke languages nobody else understood." The waitress put her hand on Jude's thigh. "Though under the right circumstances we don't have to speak at all."

"For a fish lady, you're awful handsy."

"My kind is known for going after what we want," she whispered in his ear. "I bet you've never met another woman like me before."

"That's a hundred percent accurate."

Jude leaned in for a kiss.

"What the hell are you doing!" The waitress shot up from the booth, protecting her face with her hands.

The bartender—armed with a club, a cudgel, and a truncheon—came over quickly to assess the situation. "What's going on here?"

The waitress buried her head in the bartender's chest. "He tried to bite my face off."

The bartender glared at Jude. "Is this true?"

"I...I just wanted to ki...kiss her," Jude stammered.

The waitress turned to look at Jude with tears in her eyes. "Why would you want to kill me? I was being nice to you."

"No, not kill...kiss."

The bartender shook his head. "I don't know what that is, but we don't allow no kinky stuff in here."

The cowboy returned to the table. "Whoa, what's going on?"

The waitress pointed at Jude. "He tried to kill me by eating my face."

Jude looked to the cowboy. "Kiss...not kill."

"They practice cannibalism where you're from?" asked the cowboy.

"Some used to I suppose, but I'm no cannibal," pleaded Jude. "You have to believe me."

"That's just what a cannibal would say," accused the waitress.

"We've got strict rules against anthropophagites in this establishment; it's bad for business." The bartender extended a tentacle toward the door. "You two will have to leave. No more monkeys in this bar. You're both banned for life—*simia non grata.*"

Chapter Fifteen

The two men trudged up yet another dune. The cowboy looked back when he reached the top and stared wistfully into the distance. "I'm sure gonna miss that bar."

"Once again, I'm sorry," Jude replied. "How many times do I have to say it?"

"I'll let you know when you're getting close to the right number."

"You're certain there's not another tavern, restaurant, or inn anywhere on this whole planet?"

"Not a one. There's no reason to live anyplace else on this sphere except at the bottom pole where all the stuff lands that you can collect for money, and the Taproom has the one and only Leaky." The cowboy took a sip from his canteen. "I think we're past the equator now."

"Already? We've only been hiking for a day."

"I told you, this here planet is solid but small, like a diamond covered by a kilometer-thick layer of coarse silicate."

"A diamond in the rough in the sky."

"Anyways, we should be at the top pole sometime tomorrow."

"How will we know when we get there?" asked Jude.

"I reckon things flying off into outer space will be a pretty good clue."

"Then I guess we can kiss our asses goodbye."

"Why would we bite our own asses?" asked the cowboy.

"Again, kissing is not the same as biting. It was all a big misunderstanding. I can't imagine what would've happened if I had tried to hug her."

"What's that?"

Jude stretched out his arm into a ring. "It's when you put your arms around someone."

"She probably would've torn off your arms and beat you to a pulp with them." The cowboy screwed the cap back onto his canteen. "I sure would've like to have seen that improv show."

~ * ~

The two marched in a trance-like state, having traversed more dunes than they could ever hope to count. The dunes stretched out endlessly in every direction, rising and falling like perpetual waves lapping a beach, as if they'd been trekking along some sandy shoreline only to be pushed back time and time again by the tide.

"Are you sure we didn't make a wrong turn at the equator?" asked Jude. "All these dunes are starting to look familiar."

The cowboy looked overhead. "No, the sol's right where it's supposed to be. We're still headed toward the top pole, though I admit I thought we would've made it there by now."

"I'm so exhausted from walking I feel like I'm standing still while the sand moves beneath my feet." Jude looked down at the ground. "Hey, the sand's moving beneath my feet!"

"I'll be...yep, it's moving all right. We must be getting close."

The two briskly climbed the next dune to see from the top what looked like a rainstorm of sand off in the distance.

"It's sucking the silicate right off the planet," observed the cowboy.

"I guess that means there's nowhere to go but up."

The two jogged down the dune toward the sandstorm, feeling more buoyant with each step. When their feet began to lose purchase, they could see patches of diamond coruscating from beneath the ascending silicate. Jude shouted as he saw the cowboy rising into the air ahead of him, but he couldn't hear his own words over the noise of the sandstorm and as he himself rose he could no longer see.

Chapter Sixteen

Jude landed with a great splash. He kicked his feet in a scissor motion and swam toward the water's surface. He continued to swim and soon felt the ground under his feet. He began walking out of the water toward the shore. A figure lay on the beach. *Great, more sand*, thought Jude.

The figure sat up as Jude approached, and Jude was confused to see not the cowboy but himself. His doppelganger looked equally surprised as he stood and touched his face. "You stole my mustache!"

Jude touched the space between his nose and upper lip to feel bristly hair. "And you stole my face."

Jude noticed that he was wearing the cowboy's duds and the cowboy his clothes. He felt the top of his head for the cowboy's hat but felt only bare skin. "I didn't know you were bald."

"Why do you think I wore that hat all the time?"

"I must've lost your hat in the water," said Jude. "And I think I might've pissed in your pants—sorry about that."

"Don't feel bad," replied the cowboy from Jude's mouth, "wait until you find out what I did in your pants. I think I went number three, so don't worry about the hat."

"Good, I wouldn't want you to wear that cowboy hat anyway, as I hear wearing hats too much can make you go bald." Jude rubbed the skin atop his new head again. "I'm going to sue someone if it turns out I'll be bald forever."

"Who are you going to sue exactly...hat makers?"

"Well, they'd better figure it out because they're going to owe me a lot of money."

The cowboy stretched out Jude's former arms over Jude's quondam head. "All things considered this ain't so bad. So we switched bodies, and we're both a little banged up...at least it seems we can't be killed in this world either."

Suddenly Jude saw his erstwhile head explode. He watched as his body toppled over. He looked up the beach to see a man in a black and white uniform with a musket rifle pointed at him. "Hands on your head or I'll blow it off like I did his."

Jude complied as he stared down at the headless corpse leaking blood into the sand. "And I was just getting used to the sight of my own face."

~ * ~

Jude's captor pulled him along the boardwalk by the rope attached to his bound hands, which were tied behind him so that he walked backwards and could only see in the direction of the beach from where they'd come.

"Welcome to Atro City," said Jude's captor over his shoulder, "though intruders never get to see much more of it than the gaol up ahead."

Every time Jude sped up his backwards walk to turn and get a forward view, his captor tugged at his leash. They passed several people along the boards, all of them dressed in black coats and white trousers that appeared to be from the colonial era, and all of them seeming indifferent to his predicament.

His captor stopped at a brick building where the boardwalk gave way to a cobbled road and banged on an oak door. "Open up! I've got another for you."

The heavy door opened. Jude turned to see a large man in a similar black and white uniform emerge from the darkness within. "Where'd you find this one?"

"Caught him as he swam ashore."

The large man held the door open wide for them. "Bring him in, and we'll string him up with the others."

Jude's captor led him into a large, high-ceilinged room where half nude men were held aloft in rows by ropes that ran between their backs and elbows. The prisoners rocked to and fro, appearing to Jude like players on the devil's foosball table.

His captor knocked him to the floor. "Pull your hands over your feet. Don't make me tell you twice."

Jude tucked his knees to his chest and moved his bound wrists under his legs.

"Stand up," ordered the gaoler. "Put your hands on your belly and stick your elbows out behind you."

Jude complied, and the gaoler threaded a thick rope through his elbows along his back, affixed the rope to a pully on the far wall, and hoisted Jude off the ground so that his feet dangled five feet from the floor. Jude did his best not to moan in agony, instead letting out a deep breath.

In one deft move, the gaoler ripped Jude's pants from his legs as if husking corn. He examined the garment. "These look like the trousers of a frontiersman. You say he came in by the sea?"

Jude's captor shrugged. "Maybe he swam out to sea up the beach and intended to swim back far enough past the boardwalk to sneak in over the wall."

The gaoler shook his head. "Intruders from Pau will do just about anything to get into Atro these days."

Jude exhaled again. "I don't know where I am or anything about your city other than it has a stupid name. I come from another place and would be glad to continue on to a different place if you'd let me go and allow me to be on my way."

The gaoler looked quizzically to the captor. "You understand what he's saying?"

"No," answered the captor. "He was talking that same gibberish when I first tied him up, but I can't make out whatever foreign language he's speaking."

"How can you morons not understand me?" gasped Jude. "We're speaking the same language, and despite your asinine accent I can understand you just fine."

The captor shrugged again as he looked up at Jude with a bemused expression. Jude released a stream of urine that dissolved that expression from his face. The captor drew a large knife from his belt and grabbed for the offending appendage, but the gaoler held his blade hand before he could make a cut.

"The magistrate will be here soon for fresh recruits," said the gaoler. "He'll be displeased if our latest offerings have open wounds."

The captor reluctantly sheathed his knife and dabbed at his face with a handkerchief. "I suppose being chosen for cannon fodder is far worse punishment than I could mete out."

The gaoler patted the captor on the back as the two exited the room. "Not that hanging around here is any sort of vacation. Next time though, I recommend not standing directly in front of the prisoner."

Jude released an anguished moan when the door closed behind them.

An old man hanging from the rope nearest to Jude raised his head. "It never stops being painful, but eventually you'll stop feeling the pain. Your body will soon realize there's no point in continuing to register the hurt."

Jude turned his head toward his fellow captive. "I understand you. Do you understand my words?"

The suspended captive nodded. "Yes, we all speak the same language."

"Then how come they couldn't understand me? Is it my accent?"

"No, it's their xenophobia. They can't accept that any outsider could possibly speak their same tongue. It's just who they are. These fools make themselves feel better about their benighted city by thinking anyone who washes up on its shores or shows up in the surrounding forests not wearing their uniform is beneath them. By the way, nice maneuver there, pissing in his face like that."

Jude noticed other men around the room nodding and grinning their approval. "Yeah, I kinda figured he'd just move out of the way."

The old man shook his head. "Again, for them to move would mean that a contemptible outsider was capable of causing them injury, which they simply can't abide."

"How long do they keep us strung up like this?" Jude grimaced. "I'm not sure I can take much more."

"They lower us once a day for feeding and exercise, which consists of squatting and running in place. Then it's right back up toward the rafters. We also get treated to daily showers when they spray us down and let the runoff water rinse away all the droppings on the floor below. It's as cruel as it is ingenious—no one's ever escaped."

"This is an awful existence."

"You get inured to it...and it usually doesn't last for more than a week."

"I'm sure I won't like the answer, but why not?" asked Jude. "Does it have anything to do with Pau?"

The old man craned his neck to get a better look at him. "I didn't recognize you from the woods, so I assumed you were from Pau City?"

"No, I'm not from paucity or atrocity. I'm from a faraway city that isn't something out of an old-timey nightmare."

The old man sighed. "Life in Atro City and Pau City are indeed nightmarish. Hunger and deprivation are rampant, which is why most of us, until our recent imprisonment, lived in the land between the two walled cities where we can hunt and forage, though capture by either side is a constant threat."

"Why not move faraway from both cities?"

"This valley is bounded by mountains on either side and seas at both ends. There's nowhere else to go."

"So I take it that the Pau and Atro are at war," said Jude.

"You really are from very far away. The whitecoats and the blackcoats have been fighting for as long as anyone can remember—both sides evenly matched...that is, until recently."

"What's changed?"

"It's told that a stranger, also from far away, recently took up residence in Pau, and he's been inventing devices to help them win the war. His latest invention is a cannon capable of wiping out a dozen soldiers with a single blast."

"A dozen," Jude said, "that doesn't seem like so many."

The old man looked around. "There's not many more of us than that here now. As you heard, the magistrate is coming soon to impress those of us who can stand into military service for their weekly skirmish."

"Weekly skirmish? You mean the two sides have a battle every week?"

"Yes, and until lately most clashes ended in a draw, with each side suffering roughly the same casualties, but since the whitecoats have been bringing their new cannon to the battlefield, the outcomes have been decidedly in their favor, which is why the blackcoats have resorted to impressment of prisoners to fill their ranks."

"If the city of Pau has been victorious week after week, why doesn't the Atro army sue for peace?"

"Neither the whitecoats nor the blackcoats would ever capitulate. They're too jingoistic. They'd sooner send every able-bodied man in the city, or at least men who can stand, to slaughter than surrender. It's simply their way."

"Their way sounds like suicide, which it seems they deserve."

All heads capable of turning turned when the door to the gaol room opened. The gaoler entered with, who Jude assumed was, the magistrate followed by a young man in a clean black coat and creased white trousers.

"Hear me dogs," barked the magistrate, "today is your lucky day. You have the privilege of being reviewed by Atro army's newest captain. Those of you who he sees fit will be made soldiers under his capable command for today's combat and what I'm certain will be a glorious victory for our fair city."

The young captain looked to the gaoler. "Lower these maggots. Let's see which of them has the strength to stand."

"I'm confused, are we maggots or dogs?" Jude asked as his toes touched the stone floor.

The gaoler glared at Jude. "I told you before, we don't understand your mongrel tongue."

Jude relaxed his shoulders as the rope went slack. "Okay, dogs then."

"We just got this prisoner in today," reported the gaoler. "An odd one,

106

he is."

The captain eyed him closely. "He'll do for our purposes."

Jude continued to stand as the gaoler lowered the other captives, all of whom likewise stood. The captain inspected each standing prisoner as the gaoler continued to lower the rest. The old man was last to be lowered, and after initially falling when he reached the floor, he then feebly stood.

"I count thirteen standing men," the captain announced. "Under the strict rules of engagement, I can only lead twelve soldiers onto the field of battle, so one of you will have to await your turn until next week."

The old man wobbled and collapsed.

"It seems we have a volunteer to stand down," said the magistrate. "Gaoler, we'll take the twelve who've remained standing. You may execute the layabout, since by the look of him I doubt he'll survive until next week. I'm sure you'll have new prisoners very soon."

Jude whispered to the old man, "Get up!"

The old man tried to rise once more but could not muster the strength, and so whispered back. "Don't fret over me. It's death either way."

The gaoler approached the old man with a flintlock pistol and shot him through the heart. Jude watched as his body crumpled to the floor.

The captain threw a pair of tattered white pants at Jude's feet. "You maggots put on these trousers. It wouldn't be proper to march you down the street with your dangling bits hanging out. You'll get your black coats and your rifles on the battlefield."

The dozen prisoners dressed and exited the room in a single-file line.

~ * ~

The young captain marched his twelve reluctant recruits along a sylvan path into a clearing surrounded by thick foliage. He stopped at a small cannon located on one side of the long field and turned to address his shabby soldiers. "Halt!"

With a keen eye, the captain assessed the far end of the field and saw that it was empty of whitecoats. "The cowards are late—afraid to receive their just comeuppance, no doubt."

With much consternation and fussing, he ordered his soldiers into four rows of three, then three rows of four, and finally two rows of six, which seemed to satisfy him. Then he opened a large trunk near the cannon, from which he produced twelve blood-stained black coats and a dozen well-worn rifles. "Each of you will be issued one coat and one rifle. You will receive instruction on how to load the rifle by me after you are fully in uniform. Any man who breaks rank will be shot by me. Any man who falls down had better be dead, or you'll be shot by me."

Being at the head of the front row, Jude received his coat and gun first. He pulled on the oversized coat as he espied the cannon at the opposite end of the field. The opposing cannon appeared to have many holes around a solid center rather than a single hole in the middle. "Captain, that isn't a cannon over there. It looks like a Gatling gun. It'll mow us down no matter which way we stand."

The captain promptly returned to Jude and slapped him across the face. "I don't speak your inferior language, so do not dare to address me." He snatched the rifle from Jude, removed its ramrod, proceeded to load the long gun, and tossed it back to him.

"Okay, I'll address you in a language that you can understand." Jude shot the captain in the face, and he keeled over dead into the tall grass. Jude turned to his fellow captives. "Look, I don't know what's going on here, but these idiots are still using flintlocks, and they've got a damn machine gun over there."

A stunned prisoner continued to stare at the body on the ground. "You shot the captain."

"I sense that you're not hearing me," said Jude. "We'll die if we stay here, so I suggest we scatter into the woods."

"Wouldn't it be cowardice to run?" asked another prisoner.

"They're gonna kill us with their anachronistic cannon if we don't." Jude looked over his shoulder as a war drum could be heard approaching from the footpath at the opposite end of the field. "If you're all so eager to fight, shoot down the opposing army when they arrive. The woods offer a lot of cover, and their cannon doesn't appear to swivel all that much, so you each should be able to get off a shot or two before they can return fire."

"Ain't that sort of unfair to shoot at the enemy while hiding amongst the trees?" another prisoner asked.

"It's what our captain would've wanted. I'm certain of it. Now go!"

The twelve fled with their rifles into the surrounding woods just before the whitecoats took the field.

"The cowards are late," said the captain of the whitecoats. "Afraid to receive their just comeuppance, no doubt."

Two of the soldiers readied the Gatling gun when a pair of shots rang out from either side of the field. The two soldiers fell, slumping over the barrel of the large gun. The captain watched in horror as the salvo continued, relieving him of his command in the most prejudicial way until at last he himself was relieved of his head.

~ * ~

The aged tower guard raised the gate for the captain of the whitecoats and the eleven soldiers who followed him.

"Another victory this week, I take it," called down the tower guard.

Jude tilted the captain's tricorn hat to answer the guard above. "Yes, we thoroughly routed those maggoty dogs, which our non-dead presence here clearly attests. I doubt you would've opened the gate for a lone captain who escaped the battlefield unharmed when all those under his command had perished."

"I should think not," replied the elderly tower guard as he surveyed the troops from above, "but you appear to be a man short."

Jude nodded solemnly. "Alas, I'm afraid our glorious victory came at a cost. We lost one of our own on the field of battle. Took a bullet right to the face, he did."

"I'm sorry to hear it lads." The tower guard removed his hat to reveal a hoary head of hair. "A few of your soldiers' coats look more crimson now than white."

"It's not their blood," Jude stated.

"Ah, hand-to-hand combat. I remember those days well."

"Yes, we had to engage the enemy at close range as the new cannon malfunctioned," said Jude, "which is why I must speak to its inventor posthaste."

The tower guard pointed across the lane that ran along the interior of the city's wall. "He's in his workshop at the blacksmith's."

"Thank you, good sir." Jude turned to address his troops. "And thanks be to you brave men also. You fought courageously today. Now please return to the battlefield to retrieve our fallen comrade."

"Why didn't you bring him with you?" asked the tower guard.

Jude cleared his throat. "Uhm...these fine men didn't want to further sully their uniforms, which they wear with such pride, so they insisted that we return here to take them off before completing the untidy task."

"Why didn't you have two of your soldiers remove their coats to carry the fallen hero and have another soldier carry their coats?"

Jude coughed into his fist. "Under normal circumstances that would've been a perfectly reasonable thing to do; however, most regrettably our brother in arms was mercilessly hacked into exactly eleven pieces, so the messy chore will require all of my men."

"I thought he was shot in the face."

Jude shook his head. "Hacked...then shot...then hacked at some more. Verily, it was a grisly affair that I dare not speak of further."

"I understand, but surely your boys must be thirsty after such a pitched engagement. Why not just send back a couple to collect the pieces in a sack or some such and let the rest retire to the tavern for some much-deserved refreshment."

Jude nodded for a long moment. "Yes...we discussed that very idea on the march here, but these soldiers were quite close with the dearly departed, and to a man they insisted upon sharing in this unpleasant undertaking, each carrying his own piece of their fellow soldier."

The tower guard wiped his eyes. "Good boys, them."

"Indeed." Jude turned to address his eleven soldiers. "Now remove

110

your coats and pile them neatly before leaving on your most sorrowful errand. I shall speak to the cannon maker forthwith."

~ * ~

Jude ducked into the blacksmith's shoppe, expecting to find a stout man in front of a fire, pounding hot iron on an anvil with a heavy hammer. Instead, he found a small, bespectacled man studying schematics at a writing desk, using the warmth of the blacksmith's fire to dry some socks. "Can I help you?"

"My horse threw a shoe," Jude replied.

"I hope you ducked." The bespectacled man grinned. "I take it you're a fellow traveler."

Jude removed his tricorn hat. "What gave me away?"

"For one, your accent is all wrong." The man stood from his desk. "Also, and it's a minor detail, they don't have horses here."

"Ah, now that you mention it, I haven't seen any horses since I arrived."

The bespectacled man approached Jude for a closer inspection. "Where are you from?"

"Earth, by way of the diamond world...by way of the Liminal realm."

"Strange, I've never heard of any of those places."

"Where are you from?" asked Jude.

"My home planet is known as Firma. I am...was an inventor there."

"What are you doing here?"

"I invented a portal. We have something of a migrant problem on my world. I was attempting to find a hospitable place for them to go when I got myself stuck here."

"So your portal device broke, and you can't find the parts you need to fix it in this backwards time."

The inventor shook his head. "No, my portal works just fine, or at least as well as it ever did. The problem I discovered when I stepped through it is that you can't step back...or rather you can, but you don't return from whence you came. Instead, you arrive somewhere altogether different. I stepped through on my home world into a planet with a noxious atmosphere and a very aggressive plant population. I quickly stepped through again and arrived here. Yes, these people are backwards, but at least I can breathe their air, and their trees aren't carnivorous."

"If you agree that these people are backwards, why did you build them a damn machine gun when they're still using flintlocks?"

"They imprisoned me when I first arrived and tried to make me into a soldier. I'm not an adventurer like you must be, so I convinced them that I could build a special cannon to tilt the odds in their favor."

"You tilted them all right. That so-called cannon of yours might've killed me today."

"I could've built them a plasma cannon, but my intent was not to help them win the war but rather to keep them occupied with their weekly victories so that they'd leave me in peace to pursue my studies."

"Which is trying to figure out a way to modify your portal so that you can return home?" Jude asked.

"Correct."

"But what happens if the whitecoats grow bored with their once a week win and decide to launch an all-out assault on Atro City, demanding that you make them more cannons. Or maybe someone on the blackcoats' side will invent an even bigger cannon, and the leaders of Pau City will then demand that you make a bigger one still."

"Young man, don't presume to lecture me on escalation. My world barely survived its nuclear age. I know all too well the madness of mutually assured destruction, but, with a little luck, I'll solve the problem with my portal before it comes to that and sabotage the infernal machine I created for them just before I depart from this world. Until such time, I'll continue to make only enough ammunition for it to be fired once a week."

"How close are you to solving the issue with your portal?"

The inventor sighed. "A month...a year—I don't know."

"How long have you been here?"

"I last stepped through my portal this past winter."

"Where is your portal now?"

"Concealed in the woods nearby," the inventor answered. "We can go there soon under the cover of darkness if you like. The tower guard on duty today is half blind."

~ * ~

Jude and the inventor crept along the exterior of Pau City's wall. When a cloud obscured the moon, they forded the shallow river that flowed nearby. Soon they came upon a trail that led into the dense woods.

"For my own people's sake, I'm curious how your people survived their nuclear age?" asked Jude.

"We instituted a policy that any nation who deployed atomic weapons was responsible in perpetuity for the healthcare of the survivors of the nuclear blast."

"And that really worked?"

"Yes, radiation illnesses are quite expensive to treat. If you ever make it back home, perhaps you could suggest a similar policy to your leaders."

"I don't think they would go for it. We don't even offer free healthcare to our own citizens."

"And you have the temerity to call these people backwards." The inventor blew into his cupped hands. "At least they tend to their sick as best they can without expectation of remuneration."

Jude removed his coat and handed it to the inventor.

"Thank you, young man. I didn't expect it to be so chilly this evening." He slipped on the white coat, and they resumed their walk. "I assume you intend to step through the portal despite not knowing where it may transport you."

Jude nodded. "I can't stay here. I must at least try to return home."

"As I told you before, I'm not the adventurer you are. The risk is yours to take. I will not attempt to prevent your departure. The portal is just up ahead in a cave behind a small waterfall. A simple command phrase is all that's required to activate it."

"Which is?" asked Jude.

Two stealthy woodsmen stepped onto the trail and blocked the way.

"You're required to pay a toll to use this path," said the first woodsman.

"Our apologies," replied the inventor. "We did not realize this was a tollway, but I have coins in my pocket, and we'll be glad to pay so long as we may pass without incident."

"Mark his attire," said the second woodsman. "He's a whitecoat from Pau."

"That he is," replied the first.

"No, I am not a soldier," protested the inventor. "I just happened upon this coat a moment ago and wear it now only for warmth."

"I believe you speak the truth," said the second woodsman. "You don't look like a soldier to me, but pray tell, what is your vocation?"

"I am but a humble blacksmith," the inventor answered.

The first woodsman stepped forward. "The blacksmith of Pau who arrived last winter?"

The inventor nodded.

"You made the great gun that killed two of my brothers." The woodsman leveled his flintlock pistol at the inventor's chest. "Now you'll die by my gun."

A flash lit up the dark pathway. A thick smoke filled the night air. Jude watched as the inventor fell to the hardpacked dirt. He leaned down to comfort the dying man.

"De...," the inventor said with much effort.

Jude moved his ear closer. "What?"

"Rigueur," the inventor whispered as life passed from his body.

"Look," said the second woodsman. "This one has the black pants of a Pau soldier."

"Likely they were sharing the uniform," said the first as he reloaded his pistol.

Jude stood slowly with his arms raised and then quickly dashed off into the woods. The two woodsmen gave chase as Jude ran toward the sound of rushing water. Soon he found the waterfall, but he could hear his pursuers closing the distance. He slipped swiftly behind the falling water and into a shadowy cave. He couldn't see his hand in front of his face, so he felt his way along the cave wall until he touched something metallic.

"De rigueur," said Jude.

The six-foot circle set in the cave wall lit up, illuminating the void inside the gray ring with a blue light. He heard the shouts of the woodsmen over the sound of splashing water.

"Looks like he found a lantern!"

"There must be a cave behind the falls!"

The light within the ring began to pulse, as if counting down. Jude peered into the void but could only make out a swirling mist. The intervals between the pulses increased.

"It's now or never." Jude jumped.

Chapter Seventeen

Jude fell hard onto a salt flat that extended to the horizon. The air was dry and extremely warm. He noticed that the soles of his shoes were melting into a mucilaginous mess. He walked around the portal to discover that it was only a ring on one side; the other side being a solid, flat disc of gray metal with the bottom most portion buried a foot into the cracked ground. His feet were now intolerably hot. Surveying endless salt flats in every direction, he circled back to the obverse side of the portal.

"De rigueur."

~ * ~

Once more Jude landed with a splash, but this time he found himself in a lagoon rather than a sea. The cool, still water felt refreshing against his skin. As he treaded water, he turned to see the portal resting upon a ledge jutting from the base of a tall cliff. The cliff face seemed too sheer to climb up much farther than the ledge, so Jude swam for the grassy bank at the opposite end of the lagoon. As he pulled himself onto land, he noticed several small leeches stippling his bare arms. He detached the leeches, hurling them into the wooded area beyond the grassy bank.

As Jude assessed his surroundings, he heard the sounds of trees crashing deep within the darkling woods. Jude froze as he saw a leech the size of Leaky emerge from the trees. The enormous annelid appeared angry to Jude and, in his estimation, intent on doing him harm beyond merely spraying unfiltered beer in his direction. Jude dove back into the lagoon as the leech advanced in his direction. He swam swiftly toward the portal. When he reached the cliff face, he felt a swell of water as the mammoth leech entered the lagoon. As he climbed up to the ledge, he turned to see the large shadow of the leech just below the water's surface.

Jude stood precariously on the narrow ledge. Just when he shouted, "de rigueur," the leech's head and torso shot from the water below and immediately towered above him, readying itself to strike.

~ * ~

Jude flailed his arms about, splashing at the water. Then he realized that he could easily stand. He stood up to see that the portal was ensconced at the bottom of a shallow fountain. He stepped out of the fountain as passersby shot him curious looks. Nearby was a plaque that read: El Rodeo de las Aguas. *I must be in Los Angeles*, he thought. In the distance he saw a row of palm trees. *At least I know these trees won't bite.*

Jude walked around the fountain to get his bearings, trailing a circular series of soggy footprints. He marveled at the things he saw—the clothes, the cars, the opulence. He reached the point at which he emerged from the fountain just as the first of his footprints evaporated.

"Time is out of joint," said a bag lady sitting on a park bench.

Jude instantly recognized the woman's voice and approached her. "You and I have met before...in another place and time."

"When you really start to see the future, the present begins to look a lot like the past, but no, you've never seen me before."

"That's technically true, but I know your voice. I last heard it in the mountains near Ushuaia." Jude sat on the bench beside her. "Not many street people quote Shakespeare, though given our proximity to Hollywood, I suppose it's possible that you're an aspiring actress looking for her big break."

"I am an actor of sorts...Shiva playing the beggar."

"Why destroy this city?" Jude looked up at the blue sky, taking note of two contrails that intersected one another far overhead. "It's such a lovely afternoon."

"For life to be sustainable, people need joy or purpose. Do you see either of those in the faces of the people walking past in this most prosperous of cities?"

"In my experience, the people with the nicest stuff are never the happiest. If you're angry with these people for some reason, why not leave them to their miserable lives? Trial by Ordeal."

The old woman grinned. "In another time I was accused of being a witch. They buried me alive—now that was a Trial by Ordeal."

"Are you one of the Liminals?"

"No, just a traveler like yourself, but I have not traveled nearly so far; however, even though my route was less circuitous, I did not have to be told that our world is not truly as it appears."

Jude leaned closer to the old woman. "How did you do it...how will you do it?"

"I've done nothing, nor will I do anything. I've been a traveler for my entire existence...like you, searching for understanding. Those who set you on your journey invited me here to witness the transition to come."

"But the bombs...we never determined what caused the explosions or precisely where they were detonated."

"The explosions you speak of are manifestations of the discontent of all the people around us."

"So when a population center grows dense enough and despondent enough—"

"It only requires the smallest of sparks to ignite," interrupted the old woman.

"Which is why the bombs only exploded in the most populated cities on the planet."

"For so many to live so closely together, new people with fresh vigor, hungry for opportunity, must be introduced to balance the hebetude of those who've lingered for too long. It's the proper way of things...at least to my understanding thus far."

"I get the sense that your understanding is well beyond mine and most others," said Jude, "but what will happen to you?"

"I'll travel on...appearing again somewhere else at some other time, walking as slowly as ever."

"Then we just wait?"

"I've been waiting my whole life, haven't you?" The old woman grinned again. "You and I are about to witness the world change."

"For the better?"

"I suppose that depends."

Jude's vision gave way to a sudden, overwhelming brightness as he felt the mustache burn from his face. "So this is dying."

~ * ~

Jude listened as a young man handcuffed to a short table in a small room mumbled. Jude glanced around the cinder-blocked room before focusing on the long mirror opposite the steel door. He didn't recognize either the seated man or the standing man. He touched the bare skin between his nose and upper lip, catching sight of himself doing likewise in the mirror. *The mustache is gone,* he thought, *at least I've got the hair on my head back.*

"I'm telling you, I don't know nothing," protested the seated man.

"What planet is this?" asked Jude.

"What?"

"What year is it?"

The young man held up his shackled hands. "Why you messin' with me?"

"Do you know my name?"

The young man shook his head. "Look, I don't know exactly what kind of drugs they was moving out of that warehouse, but I know they be pushing a lot of weight—quality shit too, and they had guns in some of them crates...mostly long guns, I think."

"That's interesting information." Jude crossed the small room and exited.

"Hey, I told you everything I know," the young man called after him. "What are you going to do for me?"

Just outside the room, Jude noticed a pair shadowy figures behind the two-way mirror. The older man nodded as the other man typed on his tablet computer.

"Good work," said the older man. "I didn't think you'd get him to talk so fast."

The other man looked up from his tablet. "He's in a hurry—got to get home for his wife's surprise birthday party. She's flying in from Idaho."

"I wish all my agents were equally as motivated." The older man turned to the tablet wielder. "Any word from the DEA?"

"They emailed to say that the product they recovered had been stepped on so many times it has hurt feelings, but the kid's story about the guns checks out. They'll send us a complete inventory when they've finished processing the crime scene."

"With the DEA's help and the kid's statement, I think we can call this one a win for the Bureau," the older man said.

The other man winked at Jude. "Or a win for Wynn in my partner's case."

Jude snapped his fingers. "Agent Wynn of atf...I mean the Bureau of Alcohol, Tobacco, and Firearms."

"You left off the E," the older man grumbled. "Can't even get my own agents to include 'Explosives' in our bureau's name."

"I read you, partner. Speaking of initialisms with the letter E, his wife's ETA is fast approaching." The other man tucked the tablet under his arm. "Boss, we'd better get going. I'm driving him home, and we're picking up his daughter from school on the way."

"I can finish up here," replied the older man. "Rush hour in L.A. is no joke."

~ * ~

"These surface streets are a joke," said agent Wynn's partner from behind the wheel. "We should've hopped on the expressway—even if only for a couple of exits, it's still got to be faster than sitting at all these lights."

Jude stared at the sky through the passenger's side window, eyeing two intersecting contrails. "Nah, it'd only feel faster because we'd be moving, but we'd be going out of our way."

"What are you getting your wife for her birthday?"

"I really don't know," Jude answered.

"Gonna buy her a present tomorrow after the party—that's a gutsy choice. Once for my ex-wife's birthday I gave her a card that told her she didn't have to buy me anything for my birthday. I thought it was clever; I acknowledged her birthday while at the same time saved us both the hassle of shopping for pointless gifts the other would probably just end up returning anyway. We got divorced pretty soon after that. When we get to your place, why don't you run out to get her something before the taxi drops her off? I can hold down the fort and play host to your guests as they arrive."

Jude shook his head. "Thanks, I'm sure I have something for her. I just can't remember what it is at the moment."

"This case has taken a toll on you, hasn't it? It's been one uncredible informant with an incredible story after another, but I think this kid today will do the right thing and testify, helping himself out in the process."

"I hope so."

"I know so." Agent Wynn's partner accelerated slowly through the intersection. "Are we gonna make it in time to pick up your daughter? I can throw the disco light on top of the car, if you want."

"No, that's okay."

"I wouldn't have to drive like I stole it, you know—just like I have to pee...really bad, maybe."

Jude peered down the cross street as they passed. "I don't think it'll matter much anyhow."

"Always by the book, aren't you? Safety first."

"I don't feel like any of these people are safe today."

"I know what you mean—all this traffic, everyone in a hurry, nobody paying attention to the road." Agent Wynn's partner glanced at his tablet on the armrest. "I downloaded this new crossword app. What's a three-letter word for marsh?"

"Bog."

"No, it's got to end with an N."

"Fen."

"I thought a fen was like a valley."

"That's a glen."

"Since you know so much, do you happen to know how to carve a watermelon?" asked agent Wynn's partner. "I've got a black diamond in the trunk for the party. The guy at the grocery store tells me they're easy to eat, but hard to ski. That's funny, right?"

"Right."

"Speaking of melons, is that nanny who watches your youngest going to stick around for the party? She seems sweet but strikes me as the type who goes into beast mode between the sheets. Me, I'm more like a la mode in the sack...at least that's what my ex used to say, but then each of her split personalities always was half crazy. She once told me that she wanted to have our kitchen remodeled, but I tell her we can't afford it, so she suggests we save some money by opting for stained-steel appliances...you know, instead of stainless-steel. Should I tell that joke to your nanny—or maybe not mention my ex-wife at all?"

"Do you sometimes wonder," asked Jude, "what if this is the last conversation I ever have?"

~ * ~

Jude awoke in a spacesuit. He reflexively lifted his hand to feel for a mustache, but his gloved fingers stopped an inch from his nose at the polycarbonate face shield. He sat up; a thick layer of silt fell from his suit. He surveyed the barren planet on which he'd been sleeping.

"Napping in the sands of time again?" asked a voice over his helmet's two-way radio.

Jude twisted around to see a similarly clad figure in the distance taking a ground reading with a long instrument. The figure waved at him.

Jude waved back. "Yeah, I must've dozed off."

"You anthropologists have it so much easier than us geologists. We have to rely on an array of devices to collect our data, but all you have to do is clear your mind, and it just comes to you somehow. I suppose that's the advantage of having an art mind over a science mind, but then I guess the disadvantage is that we know our data is factual while you can never be sure if what you see actually happened or if you're just misinterpreting your own imagination."

"You might be on to something there," Jude answered back.

"So, did you get a vision?"

"Uh, yeah...a memory from a resident of L.A. just before it was destroyed."

"This planet was called L.A.?"

Jude stood. "No, it was called Earth. What do you think happened here?"

"Not sure—best I can figure is that these...er, Earthlings somehow ignited their own atmosphere, causing the planet to become as lifeless as its moon. Any idea why?"

Jude walked toward the geologist, his steps labored by the weight of the suit. "Perhaps they decided to make their planet uninhabitable to forestall an alien invasion."

"Possibly, though not the wisest of strategies."

"I believe the people who lived here sometimes employed scorched-earth tactics as a last resort."

"Curious...be sure to make a note of that in your report."

"How long ago do you think it happened?" asked Jude as he approached the geologist.

"Long before our people started exploring exoplanets." The geologist pulled the instrument he'd been leaning on from the ground and turned toward Jude. "I've collected all the samples I need. Are you about done here?"

Jude stifled a gasp at the geologist's purple skin. He could see by his reflection in the alien's face shield that his own skin was likewise purple. "I want to try for one more vision."

"As you wish, but we've got five more planets to inspect before we leave this system."

"Understood," Jude replied.

The geologist hoisted the long instrument over his shoulder and turned in the opposite direction. "I'll see you back at the lander."

Jude sat down in the sand as he watched the geologist walk away. He focused on the liminal space, but when he opened his eyes, he still only saw sand in every direction. His perplexity felt as ponderous as his cumbrous spacesuit.

Should I head to the lander and leave for Mars?

Jude stood again and set off in the direction of the geologist's footprints. *Maybe being an interplanetary traveler is the life for me. I'm not sure I feel a connection anymore to this barren world.*

The toe of Jude's boot hit upon something hard. He knelt to inspect it, brushing away the sand around the pointed object. Soon he revealed the tip of a pyramid. Then once more he had the sensation of falling far and fast.

Chapter Eighteen

Jude turned his head from side to side, surveying the liminal space, which somehow seemed smaller than before.

"Are you comfortable?" asked the trespasser.

"It's nice to be out of that suit."

"What suit?"

"Never mind," Jude replied. "So then it's pure serendipity that I ended up back here?"

"Likely not. You must've unwittingly navigated yourself back into this reality; perhaps you have a stronger desire to return to your home than your predecessors. We suspect when we revealed to our previous travelers that their reality was fabricated, they lost interest in returning, but despite you being aware of its inauthenticity your world seems to hold more sway over its inhabitants."

"Thanks to you my fake world is on the verge of ruin...and I live alone. I'm in no particular hurry to get back to it, though based on my travels I doubt there's anyplace I'd rather be."

"And what did you learn in your travels?" asked the trespasser.

"That as far as I can tell, it's dipshits all the way down, and you might be the biggest dipshits of all if your greatest concern is your place in the whole mess."

"That's an interesting perspective."

"I'm pleased you think so."

"Then with your new, and I'm sure hard-earned, outlook in mind, how would you suggest we reinvest our energies?"

"By not worrying so much about where you are, but rather where you're going, and how we can all get there together."

The trespasser sighed. "I'm disappointed with your report. We were expecting a bit more elucidation from someone who'd returned after traveling so far."

"I'll do my best to get over your disappointment...hold on, I just did. I'd wager that in all the simulations you have running, the most revered leaders in each basically espouse the same principles— the best version of yourself is the one that cares more for others, the key to living well is to help others live well, treat people how you want to be treated, respect one another, live and let live

You know, there's a reason for all that overlap."

"A notion worth considering."

"Whatever...I did what you wanted—a deal's a deal. Now put me back in my reality."

"Even though you know it to be artificial?"

Jude nodded. "It's real enough for me, and I assume as a courtesy for my service that you'll refrain from further interference, allowing my reality to continue on as if you didn't exist."

"That is acceptable to us, as your reality is no longer of any consequence. We can make no significant changes to a simulation already in progress, such as undoing the destruction of your planet's six largest cities, without corrupting the entire sim; however, we can make minor alterations. As a personal favor to you, we could alter your reality so that you can retain your recently restored vision?"

"No, that's okay...but I do have one request."

~ * ~

Agent Wynn completed her second circuit of the pyramid, having reversed directions the last time in case Jude had been following behind her. She had called out to him repeatedly, but the winds were too intense for her voice to carry far. She reluctantly pulled her radio from her pack.

"Station Hielo, this is Agent Wynn. I need a search party dispatched immediately to the pyramid. I've lost—"

126

"Agent Wynn," a crackling voice interrupted. "We have a copter enroute to retrieve you."

"No, I don't need to be picked up, I need help finding—"

"Ma'am, Jude's at the station. One of our pilots spotted him wandering around halfway between your position and here. He's not sure how he got there, but other than a little frostbite, he's safe and sound. He asked me to convey a message. He suggests you return home, as you're long overdue for a birthday party with your husband and daughters."

Chapter Nineteen

Jude sat with MT in a small conference room at the United Nations Headquarters, waiting to be called before the General Assembly.

MT sniffed at the air. "What's that smell? It's an earthy scent, but it also reminds me of the ocean."

"Ambergris," answered Jude. "It comes from sperm whales."

"Ah, and since they're practically extinct, there's little chance of a trespasser ever guessing that particular scent."

"You're starting to get the hang of this."

"Thanks." MT looked from the ceiling vent to the beige walls to the brown carpet. "This is my first trip to New York, and so far all I've seen of it are the airport, a taxi, and this empty room."

"That's more of it than I've seen," Jude quipped.

"Right, because you're blind. How do I keep forgetting that?" MT rolled his eyes.

"I saw that."

"So what are you going to tell the Assembly?"

"I haven't quite made up my mind yet. What would you suggest?"

"Part of me wants to answer 'the truth,' but since no one knows what you discovered down in Antarctica, I can't be sure that's the best course of action."

"As I say, you're getting the hang of this."

Jude's phone buzzed on the table. MT looked at the screen. "You got a text."

"Are they ready for me?"

MT shook his head. "It isn't from the Assembly...says Unknown Sender. Want me to get your Bluetooth so you can hear the message?"

"No, just read it to me."

MT took up the phone and opened the IM. "It reads: 'Salutations from your Chinese counterpart. I saw you enter a moment ago. I'm in the conference room across the hall.' Do you want me to write back?"

"Yes, we should respond with something clever—how about 'hello.'"

MT typed in the word and waited for a reply. "'I've read up on you. We're similar opposites. You're descended from the talpine monks. My antecedents were octopine monks. They, like me, can't hear. I sometimes feel as if I ought to both apologize to and for my ancestors.' I didn't know octopi are deaf."

"It's octopuses. The origin of the word octopus is Greek, not Latin, so it's not pluralized by using the letter 'I'."

"Okay, so do you want me to send him another text or not?"

"Her, I believe—similar but opposite. Write: I sometimes feel the same way too. How were your travels?"

"Seems kind of mundane to ask about her flight here, but then I'm just the messenger." MT typed the question and waited again. "Whoa, talk about a non sequitur. 'Did you happen to smell anything on your journey?'"

Jude rubbed his brow. "Reply: Now that you mention it, no. I was so focused on being able to see for the first time that it never occurred to me that I couldn't smell."

MT hesitantly sent Jude's message. "I get the sense that you two aren't talking about air travel. Should I be privy to this conversation?"

"I don't see why not."

MT looked down at the phone. "She wrote back: 'Same here. Fixated on hearing, I mean. Were we merely trespassers ourselves, hopping around from sim to sim?' Does she mean sim as in simulation?"

"Yes," answered Jude. "Tell her: Could be. In such situations, I think it prudent to believe none of what you hear and only half of what you see, then to disregard the other 50 percent if you can't smell anything. All I know for certain is that the Liminals gave me their word they would no longer interfere in our sim."

MT stared expectantly at the phone's screen after he sent the message. "New text: 'They told me the same. Now the question is, what do we tell the world?' Holy shit, Professor."

Jude nodded. "Indeed. Write this: I suggest we both lie and simply tell the Assembly that we reached an accord with the trespassers. They won't return so long as we keep our promise to dismantle the planet's fossil fuel infrastructure and nuclear weapons arsenal. People don't need to know that we're living in an unreality. If they did, by tomorrow they'd've conflated none of this being real with none of it mattering."

MT tapped the send icon. A moment later a response came through. "Agreed."

The Dolor of Intermediate Tragedies

By Wes Payton

Chapter 1

"Nine out of ten metaphors can be invalidated by slippery slopes, apples to oranges, or statistics."

My uncle had been hectoring me through the long states about my decision to major in creative writing after my gap year.

"That's what you should be majoring in."

"Apples and oranges?" I ask.

"No, statistics. A statistician can do anything."

"Like climb a slippery slope?"

"You're not being serious. I'm trying to have a serious conversation with you about your future, and you're not taking me seriously. If a book could actually change the world, don't you think it would've already been written by now? Do you really believe you're going to be the one to write that book?"

"I'm not trying to change the world; I'm just trying to major in something that doesn't bore me to death. I know you're looking out for me, but statistics...don't you have to be good at math for that?"

"You're good with words. Math is just language with numbers instead of letters." He pulls off the two-lane byway onto a gravel driveway and proceeds slowly toward an old farmhouse atop a hill.

"What about algebra—that has letters...and so does geometry: A squared plus B squared equals C squared, don't you know?"

Uncle parks in front of the steps leading up to the veranda. He listens to the raindrops pelting the roof of his old Caddy before turning toward me. "My brother was a smart ass too, so I know where you get it from. I wish he was still around so that he could set you straight. He'd've told you a joke and then explained why it's better to study statistics or medicine or whatever instead of majoring in make believe...and it would've made sense to you, too—more sense than I can manage."

"You're doing okay."

"Okay." He gives me an avuncular smile and then looks through the windshield at the house and the surrounding farmland. "Jesus, this place reminds me of the black and white scenes from *The Wizard of Oz*. Are you coming in or staying out here? The choice is yours, but if you choose to come in you have to take it seriously. There's a dying lady in there who's depending on us to help her with what comes next."

I pull the kitschy kitten barrettes from my hair. "I'll come with you."

"Good." He opens his door but pauses for a moment as the arm of his coat soaks through with the rainwater. "You could always skip college and be my apprentice for a few years. The world will never run out of dying people, and I can't do this forever."

I set the barrettes in the cupholder. "I know you help these people, but I'm not so sure I believe in what you do."

"That's the thing with faith...you don't need it so much when you're young, but when you're old and you don't have anything else—then it really counts."

~ * ~

"So who are you?" asks the middle-aged man holding the door open for me. "His sous-chef in chicanery."

I shake my head as I enter the darkened house. "No, I make the snake oil."

"How do you do that exactly?"

"First I get a bunch of snakes, then I press them together really hard."

Uncle takes off his wet coat and surveys the room for a coatrack. Seeing none, he drapes his coat over a ladderback chair in the dining room. "All right, before we get off on the wrong foot here, there are two things you should keep in mind." He holds up his index finger for the man by the door and his dour wife to follow along as he enumerates his points. "One: I get

2

that you're skeptical. It's a common reaction to my line of work, but your mother invited me to her house, and unless you've recently secured power of attorney over her, you have no more authority in this situation than if your mother decided to spend her last days converting to Zoroastrianism or taking up skydiving, so please—for her sake—respect her final wishes."

"And what's two?" asks the missuses.

Uncle holds up a second finger. "I've already been paid."

"And how much did you bilk my mother for?" asks the man by the door.

"We always charge the same of all our clients," Uncle answers.

The missuses crosses her arms. "Which is?"

"Ten percent. It's been that way since the middle ages."

"You mean to tell me mother gave you ten percent of my inheritance?"

"Of course not," Uncle replies. "A testator's money doesn't become an inheritance for the inheritor until after said testator is deceased, so therefore your mother gave me zero percent of your inheritance...but ten percent of her fortune. When we spoke on the phone, she mentioned she enjoys taking naps in the parlor this time of day. May I see her now?"

The son takes position in front of a pair of pocket doors. "I have a few more questions."

"He's not here to answer your questions," I snap.

Uncle holds up a hand for calm. "It's fine. I'm sure you're only concerned for your mother's wellbeing, but time is of the essence in these situations, so let's not tarry for too long."

"I'll get right to it then. My mother called you a foozler, which sounds to me like a bamboozler."

"That's very good," I say, "those two words do, in fact, rhyme."

My uncle holds up his hand again. "Foozler is a colloquialism for what I do; it comes from the Low German, with its roots in the Hanseatic League. Calling an intermediary a foozler is akin to calling a psychiatrist a shrink, though instead of shrinking heads we foozle about inside them. Admittedly what I do is less science than art."

"Did you say artifice?" the wife asks.

"So you what," asks the son, "give my mother pleasant thoughts before she dies to ensure a happy death?"

"There's no happiness in dying," Uncle answers. "If there were, we would unconsciously race toward it since typically there's so little happiness to be had in life. Death is but a moment; however, since it's our final moment it endures, by our perception, for all eternity. That last thought is everything we'll ever know in the afterlife. Our unconscious mind is continually preparing our final thought, using our knowledge and experiences—both good and bad—to inform it. I attempt to curate that final thought, foozling about through memories, stirring up what I believe will ultimately lead to a hereafter of contentment rather than despair."

"A very nobble profession. How come I've never heard of it until I found out my dying mother had been in contact with you?"

"Do you know what an engram is?" Uncle asks.

The son shifts his weight from one foot to another. "No."

"It's a hypothetical change in neural tissue related to memory. Scientists know, or think they know, that it exists, and yet with all our encephalic testing technology—CT scans, MRIs, PETs, and EEGs...not to mention autopsies and brain surgeries—its existence has yet to be proven. If modern medicine can't prove how memory works, and we can all agree that memory is real, why would it ever bother to prove or disprove what I do, when many of those who even know of my profession are like yourself, harboring only skepticism and contempt."

"We're just as skeptical and contemptuous of psychics," says the missuses, "but at least we've heard of them."

"Because those con artists advertise with neon lights and 1-800 numbers," I reply.

Uncle shoots me a look. "There aren't many of us in the field anymore, so it's better if we keep a low profile; however, just because I labor in obscurity doesn't mean I must also work in secrecy. If you wish, come with me into the parlor, provided of course that it's alright with your mother. You can watch what I do—see for yourself."

4

The son tilts his head. "How long does it take?"

"Sometimes hours...sometimes minutes."

The son slowly pushes open the pocket doors. "Aren't you worried that I'll steal your proprietary witchcraft."

Uncle raises an eyebrow archly as he steps into the parlor. "Why would you steal what you don't value? Besides, as I mentioned before, this is more art than science; there's no recipe—no prescribed process—for what I do."

Uncle crosses the room toward an elderly woman wearing a peignoir, napping on a chaise lounge in front of a bay window. She opens her eyes as he approaches. "When we spoke on the phone last week, you said you'd be here yesterday."

"We were waylaid by inclement weather in northern Nebraska...slowed us down a bit."

"Well, you're here now, as am I, so I suppose you've arrived in time." The woman looks past my uncle to see me standing behind him. "Who's the girl?"

"She's my niece."

"Seems a pity for such a pretty face to wear a such a sad expression." She feebly points to a stack of photo albums and a shoebox full of old letters on the coffee table. "I set out the items you requested."

Uncle takes a seat next to the coffee table in a wingback chair upholstered in paisleys. "Good, let's get started then."

Chapter 2

You're looking at something...someone—one of the people in those pictures, one of the people written about in those letters. The person you're looking at is starting to come into focus...a woman, a young woman. The woman's hair looks different than yours and her face too, but you see now that the woman you're looking at is you.

This isn't a you that's ever existed before—not a you of the past or the future. You're a young woman who's had all of your experiences, lived all of your life, but who's now stepped out from the river of time. You can walk along its banks in any direction you choose, watching the current flow into the future or turning to see the past take shape in the waters upriver.

You move toward a bend in the river where the waters are roughest, weltering over jagged rocks and fallen tree limbs. The roiling flow stirs up sediment from the riverbed, making the waters turbid. Flotsam collects along the bank, pieces of grimy plastic and splintered wood. This is the spot where you were stuck in your life—the place you feared you would never leave, living out your remaining days not ever knowing free flowing waters again. Take a long look at this bend in the river. Watch the way the water laps against the bank, as if it's trying to escape from the river only to be pulled back in time and time again, muddier after each attempt.

How long did you spend trapped in this eddy? Whirlng about over and over until you couldn't get your bearings, couldn't see where you came from or orient yourself to where you wanted to go. What was it that finally freed you from this bend in the river? How did it make you feel to be flowing again, away from the whirlpool in which you'd spent so much time spinning in place?

As you walk along the riverbank, the water begins to flow faster. You look ahead but don't see anything in the distance that would account for the water's sudden change in tempo, so you continue to walk and then you hear the sound of splashing waters. Yet still you don't see anything—nothing at all. You notice that you can no longer see the river ahead of you. You've come to a waterfall. The fast-flowing water races toward the fall, crashing jubilantly into the waters below where the river continues its course. This is where you were at your happiest. The place when your life changed the most. It was a joyful time to be sure, but also a time of uncertainty, of falling— never quite sure where you would land but knowing that landing was inevitable.

What did it feel like when you splashed into those new waters? Was it exhilarating, overwhelming? Did you even feel as if you were flowing in the same river anymore? Was it difficult to navigate the turbulent waters or did you just surrender yourself to the flow?

You climb down the steep bank and continue on toward a straight stretch downriver where the waters are calm and flow slowly. This area of the river was neither the worst part of your journey nor the most enjoyable, but it was when you were at your best. Here you felt in control of the river, flowing free and unobstructed.

This is the place in the river where you choose to reenter. You step a toe in first, and the water feels warm, tickling your skin. You lunge into the middle of the river, and the current gently twirls you around. You are buoyant. Your feet no longer touch the ground; they don't need to. The water babbles in your ear, telling you unhurriedly of its many secrets. You've never felt so at peace before. From here on you will feel just this peaceful as you continue to flow forever in the unending river.

Chapter 3

I escort Uncle out of the parlor, take his coat from the ladderback chair, and help him pull it on. He hands me the car keys.

"Is he going to be okay?" asks the son, following behind us.

"The effort wears him out is all, especially when the client transitions while he's with them," I answer. "That's why I come along...to drive him back home."

"Why doesn't he just fly?" asks the wife. "We could take him to the airport."

Uncle leans on me as we walk toward the front door. "He never flies. The potential for so many people to die simultaneously...well, you saw in there how important our collective unconscious is to the transitioning. He's afraid the signals might get tangled if too many people died at once."

"People die together all the time in wars and natural disasters," says the wife.

I open the door; it's still raining. "Usually not at exactly the same moment."

"But what about—"

"Dear, that's enough," the son says, interrupting his wife. "They have a long drive ahead of them." The son holds the door open for us. "Thank you both for coming. When my mother passed, she looked...at peace."

Uncle nods as we descend the porch stairs. "She seemed like a real nice lady."

I help Uncle into the front passenger's seat and then hurry around to the driver's side. I pull the door shut and glance at my hair in the rearview mirror. I use my hands to flatten the frizzy mess and then take the kitty barrettes from the cupholder to keep it all in place.

As I drive back toward the road, Uncle's mobile phone rings. "Do you want me to answer it?"

"Would you?" He hands me the phone from his coat pocket.

"Hello." I listen for what feels like forever. "I'll have to check with him and give you a call back...yes, I'll be in touch soon."

I set his phone in the cupholder. "There's another job."

"I'm too tired." Uncle lets out a long sigh. "What is it?"

I turn on the radio. "It should be on the news."

~ * ~

Uncle has been napping on the backseat through most of Missouri, waking every half hour or so to share insights about the family business.

"Being an intermediary isn't about helping your client find a happy death but rather satisfaction in the life they've lived, and you can't do that by focusing only on the good times. You must help them with all of it—the bad times too—so they can see for themselves that because of the hard parts, not in spite of them, they lived a truly full life. It's the fullness that's important—not so much the happiness. Remember, you can spend your whole life lying to others, but you can never lie to yourself in death."

"What if the client had one big win that defined their whole life surrounded by a lot of little disappointments that never amounted to much?" I glance over my shoulder after I pass an 18-wheeler. Uncle has already returned to the land of nod. We're about three hours away from the hospital, and I'm starting to have my doubts if he'll be up to the task when we arrive.

I pull into the next rest stop and use Uncle's phone to check the status of the patient. I'm informed by the mother that there's been no change. The end could come at any time for him. I start up the car again and return to the highway.

~ * ~

As I drive up the exit ramp, the monochromatic yellow light emitted by the overhead sodium lamps makes me feel like I'm in a black and white movie. The five-story hospital stands just off the highway. I pull the behemoth Caddy into the parking lot, feeling like I'm taking up more space than I'm entitled to. I kill the engine and twist around to let Uncle know we've arrived.

"I think you're going to have to do this one, kiddo," he wheezes.

"What are you talking about? I've never done a transition before. This one can't be my first."

"It won't be." He takes a moment to catch his breath. "You can practice on me."

"You don't sound so good. Fortunately, we're at a hospital. I'll go get—"

Uncle reaches up and grabs my hand. "I've been acquainted with death long enough to know that he's come for me now. I'll make it easy on you...talk you through the process."

"I know the process. What I don't know is if I have the gift to share someone else's mind the way you do."

"Everyone in our family has that ability. I think you may have it more than the rest of us."

I place my other hand on top of his. "What if I don't?"

"There's only one way to find out."

"I don't want you to die."

"I'm not dying...I'm transitioning."

I bow my head to rub the dampness from my eyes with the back of my hand. "I don't believe in that."

"Lucky for me, I do."

Chapter 4

"You're looking at something...someone. The person you're looking at is starting to come into focus...a man, a young man. The man's hair looks different than yours and his face too, but you see now that the man you're looking at is you. This isn't a you that's ever existed before—not a you of the past or the future. You're a young man who's had all of your experiences, lived all of your life, but who's now stepped out from the river of time."

Uncle grabs my hand. "Don't do the river. That's my thing. I've heard myself say it too many times for it to work on me. Make it your own."

I look to the dome light for inspiration. "You're a young man staring up at a tree—the tree of your life."

"That's good. Trees are good. Maybe I should've used trees too...don't forget to do the voice."

"But it's so hokey," I protest.

"I apologize if certain aspects of your family's longstanding tradition as revered intermediaries sound corny to your contemporary sensibilities." Uncle coughs and puts his head down again on the backseat.

"'Revered' seems like a bit of an overstatement, but okay...I'll do the voice."

"Thanks—and remember, you're not telling the client what they're doing; you're describing what they're doing. It's their journey; you're just the narrator."

I clear my throat.

You're staring up at the tree. Above your head is a broken branch that you remember well. You'd ventured out onto this branch years ago, thinking it looked like a sturdy limb on which to sit and look down, but when you reached the midway point of the branch you heard its wood creak and

11

crack. You scrambled back toward the trunk, but the branch broke, and you fell hard. You rubbed your backside as you looked up from the ground, cursing your bad luck...or was it that you failed to notice the limb had been rotten?

You'd picked yourself up, brushed the dust from your trousers, and began to climb once more. Now you climb past the now broken bough, farther up the tree to where the branches are shorter. You spot two limbs near each other, one a little higher and set slightly back. You think this looks like a good place to sit for a while. You move onto the lower branch, then lean back against the higher one, and indeed you are quite comfortable. You watch as a robin alights on the higher branch near a nest you hadn't seen before. The diminutive bird chirps aways as she makes herself cozy in her roughhewn nest, sounding like she's singing her song just for you. She seems to notice you watching her and for a moment holds your gaze, but then unexpectedly she flies away.

Thinking that you'd startled the bird and not wanting to frighten her away from her own nest, you continue your climb. After some time, you near the top of the tree where the branches are smaller still and farther apart. You grow concerned that perhaps you've climbed too high; maybe you'll never find a comfortable place to sit. Then, near the uppermost section of the tree, you espy four small branches—two extending out from the trunk in opposite directions below two others that run parallel to the lower pair.

You climb toward the four small branches. When you reach them, you grab hold of the upper pair with each hand and then rest a foot on each of the lower pair. Despite their small size, the branches feel strong and secure. You sit and lean forward so that the trunk of your body rests against the tree's trunk and each of your limbs rests upon the tree's four limbs. You and the tree have become as one. You sway as the tree sways in the gentle wind. You've never felt so at peace. From here on you will feel just this peaceful as you continue to sway forever in the unending breeze.

"You did well. I'm proud of you." Uncle draws a final, labored breath. "You're ready...and because of you, so am I."

Chapter 5

I'm escorted into the ICU where a distraught woman waits in the corridor. She turns in my direction as I approach. Her eyes look the way mine feel.

"When we spoke on the phone earlier, you assured me that you'd be here before midnight."

"I was. My uncle passed away just as we arrived. Checking a dead man into the hospital takes longer than you think."

"So he won't be able to perform the transitioning or whatever it's called?"

"No, because, as I said a moment ago, he's dead. If it matters, his dying wish was that I stand in for him, but honestly if you're not okay with that it's okay with me."

"I'm not okay with any of this. I'm not okay that I have to wait out in the hallway, while my dying son is on the other side of that door, because hospital rules only allow one visitor at a time in their intensive care rooms."

"I'm sorry. I can go, if—"

"No, wait...calling you was my husband's idea. Apparently, before we met, your uncle helped his mother on her deathbed. I'll let him deal with you."

She pounds on the metal door. A bespectacled nurse opens the door a little. "Yes?"

"I want to come in. Tell my husband that the intermediary has arrived."

The door closes. A moment later a man in a cardigan exits the room. The wife slips past him without acknowledgement.

"Where's your uncle?" he asks.

"He died right when we arrived."

"I'm so sorry."

"I'm so sorry for you. What happened was horrible. A teenager with an assault rifle in a school..." I run out of words.

"He's here—at this hospital. They won't tell us which room, but apparently he's expected to recover."

"God, I—"

"Do you believe in God?"

I shake my head. "I don't know."

"Oh." He straightens his sweater. "When your uncle helped my mother transition, there was another man with him. Is he available to help my son?"

"That was my dad." I shake my head again. "He died a couple of years ago."

"That's too bad. Are you qualified to help my son?"

"I'm...my uncle thought so. He wanted me to take over for him."

"He was a good man. I trust his judgement. My son may not have much longer. Let me clear my wife out of the room. He's only allowed one visitor at a time."

"Your wife mentioned that."

"It'll just be you, him, the nurse, and maybe a doctor or two will stop in. How long do you think it'll take?"

I resist the urge to shrug. "Is he conscious?"

"He can't speak, but I get the sense that he can hear us, though the doctors don't think so."

"It shouldn't take long."

"Good, my wife and I would like to spend some more time with him before the end."

~ * ~

"Just so you know, I think what you do is complete bullshit." The nurse adjusts her glasses. "I've met your kind in here before. You charlatans ought to be ashamed of yourselves."

I nod at the nurse as she continues to monitor the machines connected to the boy's head. "I understand." I take a seat in the chair next to the bed. The vinyl is still warm. "Is it okay if I touch his hand?"

"If your hands are clean," she says without looking at me. "Are they?"

I get what she's so subtly implying, but I take a small container of hand sanitizer from my purse and disinfect them anyway.

"Be careful of the IV," she warns.

I hold the tips of his fingers and begin.

Chapter 6

You're looking at something...someone. The person you're looking at is starting to come into focus...a boy, a young boy. The boy's hair looks different than yours and his face too, but you see now that the boy you're looking at is you. This isn't a you that's ever existed before—not a you of the past or the future. You're a young boy who's had all of your experiences, lived all of your life, who is now staring up at a tree—the tree of your life.

One of the machines starts to beep...then another, and another. The nurse checks each of them excitedly and turns to me. "Shut up! Stop your moronic drivel. Go out into the hall so the doctors will have room to work."

Chapter 7

The mother hugs me so hard I feel like I'm in the grip of a boa constrictor. "You saved my son. Thank you very, very much."

I take a step back. "I'm so glad he's going to be okay, but it's not because of me. In fact, I did such a poor job of helping your son transition that he simply refused to do so." The mother gives me a blank stare. Perhaps now isn't the time for levity.

The father puts a palm on each of my shoulders and looks me straight in the eyes. "Our boy is going to live. I don't know what you did, but if you hadn't done it...well, you don't have to know how miracles work to believe in them."

"Again, I couldn't be happier for the two of you...the three of you, but I—"

"What do we owe you?" interrupts the mother. "Anything—you name it."

"Uh...the fee is ten percent of the client's fortune, I think."

The father nods. "It'll take some time to liquidate that amount of our assets, but we should be able to—"

I shake my head. "No, ten percent of the client's wealth...not yours."

The mother tilts her head. "But our son is only nine years old. He doesn't have any money. He spends the cash he gets for his birthdays as soon as he gets it."

I grin. "Then I guess that makes this pro bono."

Now it's the father's turn to shake his head. "You saved our son's life. We have to give you something to express our thanks."

"Your thanks is thanks enough." I shrug. "Besides, I didn't actually do my job. As it turned out, your son didn't require the services of an intermediary after all."

The nurse coughs behind me. I hadn't realized she'd been standing there. "The doctors wanted me to let you know that you can both go in now to see him. He's wide awake and asking for you two."

The couple rushes into the room as the nurse steps in front of me. "I overheard what you said about not taking their money...or credit for the kid's recovery."

"I don't deserve—"

"You did something in there," she interrupts. "I don't know what exactly, but I do know that boy was in a vegetative state and somehow you snapped him out of it. That's not nothing."

I zip up my sweatshirt. "I was in the right place at the right time, which frankly is out of character for me. Things probably would've turned out the same if I hadn't been here tonight."

"Maybe—maybe not, but either way I was wrong about you, and I'm a firm believer that the apology should be louder than the criticism."

Chapter 8

"Welcome once again to Medical Mysteries, a podcast that explores the curious and the uncanny in our healthcare community. Today we are joined by a nurse practitioner with over two decades of ICU experience. We're glad you could be with us."

Thanks for having me." The nurse wiped the lenses of her glasses. "I listen to this program all the time."

"That's very kind of you to say. Having worked in an ICU for so long, I imagine you've seen it all."

"And then some."

"We invited you on after hearing of a recent occurrence that sounds...well, miraculous."

"I can't think of a better way to describe what happened than calling it a miracle," said the nurse.

"Please tell our audience what did happen."

"Last week we were slammed in the ICU with patients from that school shooting."

"Just for our audience's clarification, she's referring to the mass shooting that occurred in Missouri a week ago—not the more recent one that happened in Maryland. Pardon the interruption...please go on."

"Sure, I should've mentioned that my hospital is located in southern Missouri. Anyway, all our beds are full, and the staff is spread thin, but—as is so often the case with these mass tragedies—as the day transitions into night beds start to open up and the chaos turns calm...that eerie calm that comes in the small hours of the morning after a terrible event."

"I think all of us in the medical community have had that same feeling. I refer to it as taking a moment to resign yourself to the situation."

"Yes, that's a good way to put it. My moment came as I was monitoring the vitals of a fourth grader who'd been shot in the head. The doctors didn't expect him to make it through the night and neither did I. I've seen all manner of head trauma in my time, but when they're so young...when it's so senseless—"

"I understand. We all do. Continue when you're ready."

The nurse took a deep breath. "So the parents are...well, you can just imagine, but the dad wants to call in this foozler before his son...I don't know...we've all got beliefs that help us through difficult times."

"I share your skepticism. Again, to clarify for those in our audience who may not be familiar with intermediaries, or foozlers as they're sometimes referred to...they're individuals who represent that they have a unique ability to help guide the dying into a peaceful afterlife. Part mysticism, part pop psychology—my understanding is that intermediaries believe the hereafter is but a single moment at the end of one's life—that final moment—lived for all eternity, at least from the dying person's perspective. I've heard foozlers describe it as a snapshot—that last frame in the movie of one's lifetime that supposedly plays just before everyone dies. The thinking, and I use that term loosely, is that an intermediary can help make that final picture as pleasant as possible, even for an unconscious patient. I spent eleven years working in a maternity ward, and though they're not nearly as well known, I liken them to doulas...as if incense and nonsense can somehow ease life's transitions."

"I shared that same opinion," the nurse added, "shysters preying on the frightened and the desperate. But this experience last week—"

"Tell us about it."

"This young woman...this girl who couldn't have been more than twenty shows up at three in the morning. Apparently, she's the niece of the guy who was the foozler for this boy's grandmother when her time came. Anyway, she starts to do her thing—I've seen it before—lot of mumbo jumbo and hand holding...but this kid, who was a vegetable and not the healthy kind, starts to react. His EKG spikes, his eyes start moving under his eyelids, then his fingers begin to twitch. I call for the doctors, who come running, and by the time they get there, the boy is all but sitting up in bed.

I've seen youths make some speedy, unexpected recoveries before, but nothing like this. The doctors were as baffled as they were delighted. The parents were overjoyed to the point of hysteria."

"That sounds like quite a scene."

"Like something out of a made-for-TV movie...the kind of happy ending you just don't see in these sorts of situations—ever."

"How's the boy doing now?"

"He's on his way to making a full recovery. The doctors say that aside from some scarring and occasional bouts of dizziness, he should be fine physically. They're anticipating he'll be ready to go home in a couple of days."

"That's an amazing outcome."

"You want to hear something really amazing?" asked the nurse. "This girl didn't charge the parents a dime."

Chapter 9

It seems as soon as I set Uncle's cellphone down it rings again. It's been like this for over a week now. I think he's had more people call his phone since he died than he ever did while he was alive.

"Hello...yes, this is she...no, I haven't heard the podcast yet, but I've certainly heard of it...that's right, I'm his niece...thank you, he was a good uncle to me, and I'll miss him...I haven't decided if I'm taking over the family business...I understand, and I'm sorry that your family is going through a difficult time right now—I can relate—but I'm just not available at the moment...it's not an issue of the money, we never charge any more or less than ten percent...again my apologies, but I wish you and yours all the best."

I set the phone to silent and plug it into the charger on the nightstand. I pull my kitty comforter up to my nose, though I feel like this is a time for a decision...not another nap. I still sleep in the twin bed I did when I was a little girl. Meanwhile, Dad's dusty queen-sized mattress down the hall hasn't been slept on in two years. It seems I'm to inherit Uncle's house as well, making me the only nineteen-year-old I know who owns two houses—too bad I don't share their taste for wood paneling.

I'd thought of painting the walls, but despite the paneling making the rooms feel dark, I like keeping Dad's house the way he wanted. He never got his way when he and mom were together. Somehow, none of us did. Besides, my plan had always been to go away to college after taking a year off from school to drive Uncle around so that he could finally save up enough to retire. I should let the next owners paint this house how they want.

I push the comforter off me. I turn the phone over on the nightstand and look at the screen. Another call is coming in.

"Hello."

"Do you know who this is?" the man on the other end asks.

"I remember your voice. Are you the boy's father from last week—

"Yes," interrupts the voice. "Sorry if I sounded cryptic just then. What I meant was did you recognize my contact name from your uncle's cellphone."

"My uncle never used contacts on his phone. He said it was because he thought he'd never answer it if he knew who was calling him, but I think he just couldn't figure out how to enter contact information despite me offering to show him many times. How's your son doing?"

"Good. He's home now. He still has some bandages, but his hair is already starting to grow back. Thanks for asking."

"Of course." I wait a beat. "So..."

"So I'm calling because I, well, several of us parents from my son's school have a proposition for you."

"I haven't decided yet if I'm going to step into my uncle's footsteps and become the latest generation of foozlers in my family."

"That's not exactly what we had in mind. It's been long enough now that all the shooting victims are on the road to recovery or have, regrettably, passed."

"Yes, I've been following it on the news. The fatality count seems to have leveled off."

"That's one way to put it."

"Sorry, I could've said that better. I'll definitely need to work on my bedside manner if I decide to—"

"Actually," he interrupts, "for what we have in mind that won't be an issue anyone will be concerned about."

Chapter 10

I push open the door of the diner and a bell overhead announces my entry. I see the father and two women seated in a corner booth. Just like me, they drove several hours to get here. We agreed to meet at the midway point between us—a town neither I nor the father had ever heard of. The father waves as the two women study me.

The father rises from the round booth. "Thanks for coming. I hope your drive was okay."

"Yeah, I caught up on some podcasts." Unsure of whether I'm supposed to slide in next to the two women, taking the father's place, or wait for the pair to scooch over so that I can sit on the other end, I remain standing.

As if sensing my dilemma, the father resumes his seat. "We can scoot in so that you can sit on this end. After such a long drive, you may need to get up and use the restroom. We got here about ten minutes ago, so we've already had a chance to visit the facilities."

They crowd closer together, giving me almost half the curved seating area. I sit but keep my distance. "Did you order food?"

The father shakes his head. "Just coffee so far. We didn't want to be chewing when you arrived, but we'd be glad to eat if you're hungry—our treat, of course."

"Feel free, but I had a sandwich in the car."

"Us too," replies the father. "We stopped for drive thru on the way, and then I got some pretzels when we filled up with gas."

The woman nearest me rolls her eyes. "We've heard about what you did for his son. It's all anyone is talking about back home...well, not all, but it's the one good thing anyone talks about."

I nod. "I'm not sure I really did anything, but I was glad I could help.

Before last week, the most important thing I ever did was find my neighbor's missing cat. It was dead under our porch."

"We also heard that saving the dying isn't what you people normally do," the woman continues. "You assist people in transitioning into the afterlife. Do I have that correct?"

I nod again. "More or less. They'll transition into the afterlife regardless of our assistance, but what we do is help frame that experience for them. Although, I haven't decided if I'm going to go into the family business yet. I was just filling in for my uncle last week, who passed away, as you probably heard. It was his dying wish that I fulfill his commitment."

"I'm sorry for your loss," says the farther woman.

"Thank you. I know it's not a competition, but he was old and overweight. What I'm going through must pale in comparison to what your community has endured recently."

"Yeah," says the father. "They both lost a child last week—a son and a daughter."

The waitress approaches. "Can I get you something, miss?"

"Not right now, thanks."

"Not even something to drink—coffee...a soda perhaps?"

I turn to the waitress and realize she isn't asking me if I want anything, but rather suggesting that I should order something to pay for my place at the table. "Do you have pie?"

"We make the best pecan pie in the county."

"Great, I'll have a slice of that. Does anyone else want a slice too?"

The two women look at each other and then nod.

"I can't remember the last time I had pecan pie," the father says. "I think we'll all have a piece."

"Excellent decision," replies the waitress. "I'll get that order in for you right now."

I turn back to the father. "You piqued my interest when we spoke yesterday on the phone, and I appreciate you filling me in on some of the details that haven't made the news, but—"

"Judging by the media coverage," interrupts the nearest woman, "our mass shooting seems like a footnote to what happened in Baltimore last week."

The farther woman takes a deep breath. "Even though the death toll was nearly the same, what happens in big cities always takes the headlines."

"But what?" asks the father.

It takes me a moment to remember my 'but' after having shifted gears to consider small town news reporting. "Oh...but what's your ask? I mean you asked me here, but I still don't understand why."

The father exhales. "As I'm sure you can imagine, all of us parents who were affected by the school shooting have become closer—close even for a tight-knit community like ours. Over the last week I've been asked many questions about intermediaries. My family always knew of foozlers; I thought most families did, even if they didn't call upon their services, but apparently what you do isn't common knowledge."

"Can you really 'frame,' as you put it, a person's afterlife?" asks the nearest woman.

I concentrate on keeping my shoulders from shrugging. "Of course, it's impossible to know for certain, but my father always said a eulogy was for the mourners and what our family did was for the dying. I believe what we do gives comfort."

"Then can it also give discomfort?" asks the farther woman.

I squint as if to focus my hearing. "Pardon?"

The father shoots the farther woman a look of admonishment. "The plan was to broach our 'ask' a bit more gradually...ease into it a little, but it's been a trying week, and patience is at a premium."

Despite not having poured anything into her mug, the nearest woman begins to stir her coffee so stridently that the metal spoon clangs against the ceramic. "That son of a bitch who killed our kids—gunned down children he didn't even know—was released from the hospital into police custody yesterday, and he's going to be arraigned the day after tomorrow, since now they finally know how many murders they can charge him with. Apparently, he intends to plead guilty. Apparently, this piece of shit teenager is in some sort of online cult and can't wait to die."

The father nods. "Given the severe nature of his crimes, as well as him signaling his intention to plead guilty and refusing legal counsel, the district attorney is inclined to honor his wish and seek the death penalty."

"He's proud of what he did." The farther woman dabs at her eyes with a napkin. "He's a hero to these online degenerates...anonymous animals who've been posting the most vile things about our—"

"His mother was a piece of shit too," interrupts the nearest woman. "Probably birthed him out of her own asshole, which just proves that shit doesn't fall far from the—"

The father takes his turn to interrupt. "I don't think what's being said now is constructive, so let's get back on track here. This young man is remorseless, and none of us want him to die thinking he's some kind of martyr who's destined for an afterlife in paradise with...well, whatever teenage psychopaths imagine paradise to be. I've spoken to a lawyer, and she informed me if he does plead guilty and he is sentenced to execution that opportunities to visit inmates on death row are strictly limited to family, clergy, and attorneys; however, if you posed as a friend, she could arrange for you to see him before he's arraigned."

I blink hard and then blink again. "You want me to meet with this creep...and do what exactly?"

The nearest woman takes the spoon from her coffee. "Twist his already twisted mind so that he dies hating himself for what he did."

I shake my head. "That's not at all what I do...not what anyone in my family has ever done."

"Keeping people from dying also isn't what you do, but you saved my son." The father reaches out and places a hand on my shoulder, seemingly his go-to move for conveying big feelings. "My family has long believed in the cause of the intermediaries, giving comfort to the dying, but now my community is grieving, and we're asking you to give comfort to the living. You can help my family again...and all the families touched by this tragedy. You can do this."

"You believe what he did was wrong, don't you?" asks the farther woman.

"Of course, but—"

"Don't you think he deserves to be punished," interrupts the farther woman, "not rewarded?"

"Yes, but..." I pause, waiting to be interrupted again. "But how do you know that he'd even be willing to see me?"

"Because you're pretty," answers the nearest woman. "Whether he spends the rest of his life behind bars or they fry him next year, you're likely the last pretty girl he'll ever see—in this world, at least."

"My attorney can show him the article from our local paper about you, which included a photograph," adds the father. "You're not much older than he is."

I find myself wishing I had a reason to keep from speaking for a few moments. The waitress arrives with our pie.

Chapter 11

I watch from a metal bench in the concrete outer room through a window of wired glass as the father's attorney talks with the inactive shooter. He appears to be ignoring her and staring at the ceiling, though he looks my direction after the attorney slides him a newspaper clipping across the table. The lanky teen has a tattoo on his forehead that reads: Born To Die. He smiles at me.

The attorney gets up and bangs on the heavy door. The guard standing in the corner walks past me to unlock the door and let the attorney out. Then she sits next to me.

"In all my years practicing law, he's the only defendant I've ever met who doesn't want to talk to a lawyer, but he's agreed to talk with you. However, you should go in with your eyes open. Besides being a homicidal monster, he's at that age when it's really important for him to mock others. Don't let him get inside your head. You're here to get inside his. If at any point you sense that he's got the upper hand, just stand and leave. Don't give that shit heel the satisfaction. Personally, I think this whole gambit is cockamamie, but enough people seem to believe this will bring a modicum of peace to the families of the victims that my opinion isn't important."

"Me being here doesn't feel like justice," I say. "This is not what my family does—my ancestors."

"This isn't about them or about justice—it's about just us...you, me, all the grieving parents, those kids who'll never be whole again, and the ones that are gone. The law can't hurt this reprobate the way he hurt this community but maybe you can."

"So my only purpose here is to exact revenge?"

She slumps back against the wall. "Exact revenge...imprecise revenge—revenge is revenge."

"This seems like such a slippery slope."

"Don't kid yourself, kid. Issues like this never rest upon flat, unslippery ground."

I rise to my feet. "Okay, I'll try."

The attorney nods. "That's all anyone is asking."

The guard pulls open the door for me, and I enter. I take a seat in the plastic chair across the table from the shackled prisoner and refrain from making eye contact by looking around the cinderblock room. I notice that the table is bolted to the floor.

"Aren't you going to say something?" He turns his head to sneeze.

"Less you," I say.

"You're an intermediary, right? I've read about your kind online—cool job...totally bogus, but cool."

"You don't think there's any sort of life after death?"

"There's no afterlife, no reincarnation." He presses his finger emphatically against the top of the table. "There's this and then there's nothing. After we die, there will be no sense that now we're free from whatever; there won't be a now or anything at all."

"One of us is right, and one of us is you."

"You, a foozler, question my beliefs...though I suppose if everybody believed as I do then you wouldn't have any job security."

"What else do you believe?"

He starts table pointing again. "I believe too many people today have pride but no honor, and you can't truly have one without the other. I believe only god is all powerful, and I'm certain there is no god. I believe those who take chances must also take accountability. I believe all dullards behave the same; only cleverness enables anyone to do something genuinely unique. I believe real power is being able to act as you wish and to be who you are. I believe the best way to die is by lead poisoning—a bullet through the brain."

"Do you believe those children you shot deserved to die?"

"How many did I kill? They won't tell me."

"I won't either."

30

He shrugs. "I guess I'll find out tomorrow at my arraignment. Let me ask you another question. Do you believe those kids were happy a week ago before I came into their lives?"

"Yes."

"Do you think they'd be that happy a decade from now when they're our age, or maybe three decades from now when they're miserable and middle-aged, or perhaps in six decades when the only thing they have to look forward to is death. Do you think their futures would ever again offer the kind of happiness that kids playing on a playground enjoy?"

"Because of you we'll never know."

"I did them a favor. Thanks to me they went out on top. All I ask is that the so-called justice system returns the favor."

"That sounds about as stupid as a face tattoo. I'd say you're an asshole, but that'd be disrespectful to sphincters, which actually serve a purpose."

"I serve a purpose."

"Is that what they tell you in your little online cult, which seems really cool by the way."

He grins. "It's not little, and they don't tell me a thing. In this world I'm a skinny nobody—no friends, no money. In that world I'm the Miscellaneous Chieftain, the Minister of Mischief, and my followers revel in my exploits even though I tell them that every moment they spend living vicariously through me is a wasted moment they'll never get back."

I frown. "That's the thing about crazy, it never rests."

"Mine will be a short life. Why rest through any of it? Though I wouldn't expect you to understand—someone whose clientele's median age is dead. No offense, but I'm me and you're you. The ideas I have in my head are too big to fit inside yours. Anyway, aren't you here to foozle with my mind or whatever? They're not going to let us talk forever, and I'm anxious to hear for myself that voice you people do."

I clear my throat.

You're looking at something...someone. The person you're looking at is starting to come into focus...a man, a young man. The man's hair looks

31

different than yours and his face is free of markings, but you see now that the man you're looking at is you.

"I dig the voice," he says, "kind of creepy and comforting at the same time, but am I supposed to be feeling something here...I mean in my head, like?"

"I don't know what it feels like in your head, and I don't want to. I just know that usually the person being foozled feels better when it's done."

I return to the voice.

This isn't a you that's ever existed before—not a you of the past or the future. You're staring up at a tree—the tree of your life.

"Hold on a minute," he says. "It's a tree? I thought it was a desert— you know, walking through a desert and you come upon an oasis that represents the high point of your life...blah, blah, blah."

I shake my head. "My dad did deserts, my uncle rivers. We each do our own thing."

"Interesting."

You climb up to the lowest limb of the tree. It seems a good spot to sit, but when you step a foot out onto the branch it breaks and falls, so you continue to climb.

"If I'm just looking for a place to sit, why didn't I stay on the ground and pop a squat in the grass?"

"This'll work better if you don't keep interrupting," I say.

"My apologies—no more interruptions...please, foozle on."

You climb to the next branch, which looks even sturdier than the last, but again you take a step out, and it snaps, crashing to the ground. The trunk is getting narrower now, and the branches above you seem smaller, but you climb on; however, branch after branch breaks. You look down to see that the ground is littered with broken tree limbs. You look up again and see that there is one final branch above you—far above you. You climb toward it, gripping the trunk tightly as the wind starts gusting, causing the tree to sway from side to side. Logically you understand that this final branch will surely break and fall just as all the others have before, but your instincts tell you that this last tree limb is stronger than the rest. Somehow you know on that branch you will find a comfortable place from which you can watch all the world below, forever.

I stand to leave.

"Wait." He reaches toward me. The chain from his shackles keeps his wrists restrained just above the table. "That's it? Doesn't it usually take longer?"

I turn from the door. "Sometimes it takes hours...sometimes just minutes."

"Aren't we supposed to discuss my childhood?"

"I'm a foozler, not a shrink."

"But don't we also look at old photographs or something?"

"Did you bring any?"

He shakes his head. "Of course not."

"Then we're finished." I bang on the door.

"There's a fine line between leaving your customer wanting more and not giving your customer enough. I've got to say, you didn't earn your ten percent."

"We'll see about that."

Chapter 12

"For the final segment of today's episode, we're going to do something a bit out of the ordinary for Medical Mysteries. We're going to speak with someone not in the medical community. We're joined now by a smalltown attorney who was recently involved with the infamous case of the Missouri school shooter—"

"Tangentially involved," the lawyer interrupted. "I was neither a member of the prosecution team nor the defendant's appointed attorney."

"Thank you for clarifying. You being with us is something of a bookend. Several weeks ago, we spoke with an ICU nurse who described for us this intermediary who played a role in the recovery of one of the victims of that heinous crime. And it's recently come to light that this selfsame foozler also had contact with the gunman while he was incarcerated and awaiting trial."

"Actually, at that point he was awaiting arraignment, intending to plead guilty, so there would have been no trial."

"Ah, thanks again for the clarification. As you know, I'm used to chatting with folks in the healthcare field, not the legal field, so I'm a bit out of my wheelhouse."

"That's quite alright," replied the lawyer.

"You used the phrase 'at that point' a moment ago. We know, of course, there was a trial, which ended in a guilty verdict and a life sentence without the possibility of parole, but some of our listeners may not be aware that there was indeed a point when this horrible excuse for a human being wanted—even demanded—to be executed."

"Correct, he was relying on the court to fulfill his death wish."

"And it was this foozler who talked him out of it."

"Yes, I would say she likely dissuaded him from his then intended course of action," said the lawyer. "I was in the adjacent room when their conversation occurred; however, I did not overhear what they discussed."

"Nevertheless, soon after that discussion, this psychotic teenager changed his mind."

"Right, he reengaged with his appointed legal counsel, and ultimately entered an innocent plea, which resulted in the trial that revealed mitigating circumstances from his own childhood."

"As I mentioned, this all occurred in a small town. What was the reaction from members of the community, especially the parents of the victims, about this plea change and the intermediary's involvement?"

"It was mixed, as you might imagine," answered the lawyer. "Some characterized her involvement as interference and thought the defendant deserved to die. Others felt that life in prison—particularly for someone so young who'll likely live for many more years—was a fate worse than death."

"Why do you think she did it?"

"Convinced him to change his plea...I'm not sure, really. Maybe she agreed that a quick demise was too easy or that giving him what he wanted was too good for him, but I think probably she felt—having been around her family's business for so long—that death should come in its own time. Perhaps she thinks the guilty have as much right to live as the innocent. If a few are allowed to decide how and when some die...well, it becomes a slippery slope, you know?"

The Immeasurable Man

The Immeasurable Man is a sci-fi/speculative fiction story about celebrity, cryptocurrency, artificial intelligence, and the way we perceive reality, but at its core it's about a lonely individual who wants nothing more than to connect with someone. Due to a severe immunocompromised condition, IM lives a solitary life, only interfacing with the outside world through his computer screen. All he knows of human interaction is what he's seen in movies and on television, but when his tech-savvy older brother offers him a chance to have a life beyond his domicile, IM thinks his dream has finally come true. Little does he know that life on the outside is much more complicated than what he's been led to believe.

Prologue

Future generations will never believe the ingenuousness of the people I'm going to tell you about—it would strain credulity, as they say...so, for posterity's sake, let's call all of what comes next a work of fiction.

I exist in extreme isolation. I've been immunocompromised since birth, and though now in my mid-thirties, I have no memory of ever having had direct human contact. Until recently, all my knowledge of human interaction was theoretical; however, since the side effects of my sequestration were identified a couple of years back, my aptitudes have become very much in demand.

Aptitude One: Decisiveness. I don't hesitate when making decisions, and I don't second guess myself—ever. Why should I? My formative years were spent almost exclusively in study. I've seen every film worth seeing since the dawn of cinema. You learned how to be human from your fallible family, your fatuous friends, and your chucklehead classmates. I learned courage from Errol Flynn, self-confidence from Clark Gable, forbearance from Humphrey Bogart, resolve from Sidney Poitier, humor from Groucho Marx, and how to see right through someone from Bette Davis.

Aptitude Two: Detachment. Given my circumstances, this one hardly requires explanation, except to say that while being detached may not seem like an aptitude, in my case it is...or rather, it is in the cases I'm assigned. I literally have no skin in the game—my impartiality has never been questioned, rendering my decisions unassailable, which in this litigious age is advantageous to say the least. You can't sue a ghost...you'll see what I mean in a moment.

Aptitude Three: Discernment. I don't claim—though others have— to possess a particularly great mind, but I doubt you'll ever encounter a less cluttered mind than mine. Everything I know, everything I've experienced has come to me through the portal that is my domicile's viewscreen, all of which I've fastidiously categorized and catalogued. I have access—just like you—to nearly unlimited knowledge, but unlike you that flow of information isn't impeded by off-screen obligations and outside influences or encumbered by eventual disinterest. I simply have nothing else to do. My high-definition conduit to the world is all I have, and through it I have observed all.

So those are the 3 Ds of me, though I doubt my brief description has left you with a sketch that's very three dimensional—gramercy Groucho! If you'd like to understand my situation better, I invite you to spend a few days with me...everything really got started on what I'd been led to believe was the second Tuesday of February.

Act I

Chapter One

Arlo sat uncomfortably on the couch in the bank's waiting area, reading a months-old copy of Architectural Digest. His suit didn't fit well, his beard itched, his stomach was doing somersaults, his hearing aid—which he usually barely noticed—felt like it might fall out of his ear at any moment, and the pistol tucked into his waistband poked against the vertebrae in the small of his back. He thought he might've disengaged its safety when he'd sat down. Also, he had no idea what a flying buttress was despite having just perused an article about their modern usage, and he had to pee.

He furtively glanced over at his brother, Dylan, who stood near a small table lined with short stacks of deposit slips. He looked more like a loiterer than a customer. His fulsome beard and sweating brow gave him the appearance of someone who only stopped in for the free air conditioning. Dylan nodded, and Arlo turned to see the bank manager approaching.

"Good morning," signed the bank manager (translated from ASL).

Arlo stood, hoping his gun wouldn't slide down the back of his trousers. "I'm so pleased someone here knows sign language. I wear a hearing aid, but really it only allows me to hear car horns and alarms." He quickly dropped his hands, wishing he hadn't mentioned alarms.

"My daughter was born deaf, so whenever a customer comes in who signs, my employees let me know—frankly, I prefer signing to talking...the conversations tend to be less discursive."

Arlo smiled. "I quite agree...besides, so many people have unattractive faces, but ugly hands are a rarity."

The manager chuckled. "That's a good point. Follow me to my office, and we'll discuss how I can help you today."

The two walked in step along the tile floor dividing the tellers' counters from the loan officers' cubicles to the lone, walled office at the back of the bank. The manager opened the door for Arlo to enter and motioned to a wingback chair facing a double pedestal desk. Then he shut the door and sat in his desk chair. "I noticed that you were reading an architecture magazine. You may be interested to know that this bank is a converted bus station...what once was a depot is now a place to make a deposit."

"Then where does one go to catch a bus around here?" Arlo asked with gesticulating hands.

"I don't know...perhaps Greyhound has designs to convert the old Wells Fargo building three blocks over." The manger studied Arlo's face for a moment. "Have we met before?"

"I don't think so...this is my first time coming here."

"No, I know I haven't seen you in here before, but you remind me of someone I was introduced to at a benefit that I attended with my daughter a few months back—an inquisitive young man, though now I recall him being somewhat younger than you...or at least cleanshaven."

Arlo shook his head. "I'm new in town, so I'm sure it wasn't me that you're remembering."

The manager nodded. "Probably not then...so I understand you want to make a deposit with us today."

"No, a withdrawal," Arlo signed emphatically.

"Oh, I was told by the teller you communicated with that you were dropping off, not picking up. I'll access your account." The manager tapped at the keyboard on his desk. "Do you have an ID? I assume your account was set up at one of our other branches since you're new to the area."

"A sizeable withdrawal," signed Arlo insistently.

"Yes, I understand."

"I don't think you do." Arlo held up an index finger to signal for a pause as he pulled the pistol from under his jacket.

~ * ~

IM paused the viewscreen as his domicile's speaker chimed. "Hello there."

"IM, are you available for an assignment?"

"I can never tell if you're being sarcastic or courteous when you ask me that."

"Usually a bit of both."

"I didn't think that was possible," replied IM.

"Maybe it isn't, but your skill set is needed right now to address a relatively isolated situation that could escalate into a national headline if not dealt with promptly, so let's call it the latter and move on, shall we?"

"By all means."

"Good then, an attempted heist of a financial services institution located in the U.S. state of—"

"A bank robbery—isn't that a bit...mundane for me?"

"It's developed into a hostage situation."

"The local constabulary doesn't have a negotiator on staff?" asked IM.

"Your services were specifically requested by the well-connected father of one of the bank customers who's currently being held hostage."

"Okay, send me the details."

"I'm IM'ing you them now, IM."

IM studied the data on his viewscreen for a moment. "Ah, something of a quandary I see."

"It would seem the strategy of the four bearded bandits was to have two of them take over the bank manager's office, the only enclosed room in the otherwise open-floorplan building, which also happens not to be equipped with a surveillance camera, while the other two guarded the front door. Apparently, the two in the office convinced the manager to instruct his employees to gather up all the cash they could and stack it outside his office door. However, soon after they did so, the lobby cameras caught all six employees and ten customers flinching simultaneously—"

"Presumably startled by a gunshot they heard from the office," interrupted IM, "so I take it there's no audio to accompany the video files I'm seeing now."

"I'm afraid not. Why do you think they would've shot the manager after he complied with having all that money piled up?"

"Possibly because he wasn't willing to comply with their next demand."

"Which was?"

"Telling his employees to round up the customers and send them into his office," answered IM, "where I suspect the robbers intended to shave their beards and mix in with the customers when they're to be set free, mistakenly believing that their gambit could defeat the facial recognition program the authorities will undoubtedly use in an attempt to track them as they make good their escape."

"That's pretty clever...you don't think shaving their beards could fool the program?"

"Even if it could, the authorities already have all the shaven customers on video, so it would only be a matter of identifying whose faces exited that weren't captured on camera entering...besides, unless the would-be robbers intend to eat their own whiskers, they'll all either leave behind a massive pile of DNA evidence or each will make their exit with a rather incriminating clue somewhere on his person—so not clever...though I suppose it's easy enough for a strong premise to outshine the weaker points of a plot. For instance, take the movie Casablanca—"

"I did mention this is a matter of some urgency, didn't I?"

"Of course," IM replied, "let's press on."

"FYI, if the assailants are convicted of murder during the commission of an armed robbery in that state, it's a mandatory life sentence."

IM shook his head. "Which means, legally speaking, they'd be in no worse circumstances if they just started killing the hostages who've seen them and then effected their escape during the ensuing pandemonium."

"As you say...a quandary."

Something on IM's screen caught his attention. "I'm reviewing the video from the lobby before the robbery began...one assailant seems to be conversing in sign language with the bank manager."

"Is that relevant?"

"It might explain how he gained access to the manager's office without putting anyone on alert...and it gives me an idea."

"Speaking of the manager's office, I was just informed that the smoke detector in there was triggered...more gunfire perhaps?"

IM scanned the live feed on his screen. "No, I'm reading concern on the faces of the customers, not startlement like before. I think the perpetrators are burning their beard trimmings...perhaps they're cleverer than I first thought."

"If they're torching evidence, then it probably means they're about to make their move."

"I agree. Link me up to a holo-case onsite and tell the authorities to toss it through the front window of the bank, but first have them freight the case with an obstreperous item I'm sending you the specs for...or something comparable, if they don't have that particular payload on hand."

~ * ~

"There's a cop coming," shouted a bewhiskered robber by the bank's inner vestibule door. "What should I do?"

"It's just one cop?" asked another hirsute gunman keeping watch over the customers and employees lying face down in the lobby.

"Looks like it...all the rest of them are still hunkered down behind their squad cars. Should I let him in?"

"Are you nuts...tell him to piss off."

"He's carrying a case."

The gunman turned toward his partner at the front door. "What's in it?"

"Sure, let me use my x-ray vision to find out."

"I mean is it big, like a footlocker, or small, like a cigar case?"

"It's just a regular briefcase sized case...seems kinda high-tech though."

"It could be full of explosives."

"Why would the cops give us explosives?" asked the robber manning the door.

"No, I mean to blow us up."

"And kill our hostages?"

"Then maybe it's full of money."

"We just robbed a bank...we don't need money—we need a way out of here."

"As if I didn't know that." The gunman turned back to the hostages on the floor. "Wait to see what he does with it."

"He...he just dropped it off outside the front door and kept on walking."

"He didn't run?"

"No...set it down like he was delivering the mail."

"If he didn't run, then it's probably not a bomb."

The robber entered the vestibule and inspected the case through the glass door. "I think it's a holo-case."

"How can you tell there's nothing in it?"

"No, not hollow...I mean it looks like it's set up to project a holographic image."

Suddenly a life-size version of IM appeared in blue light atop the case. "May I come in?"

The robber jumped back from the door. "Oh shit, it's the Immeasurable Man."

"Here?" asked the other gunman incredulously. "Aren't we...a little beneath his notice?"

"Apparently not—he's looking right at me."

"I can hear you through the case's microphone and have access to the bank's surveillance video feed," replied IM, "but my holographic image is not 'looking' at you. In fact, I only know I'm facing you because I can see my image from the camera mounted in the vestibule's ATM."

The robber turned to the ATM on the wall next to him and then back to IM, who waved to himself. "What do you want?"

"To come inside and talk calmly with you all in hopes of figuring out a way to peacefully resolve the current situation. I promise, my incorporeal form won't attempt to overpower you...that was a joke."

The robber turned back toward the gunman in the lobby. "What do you think?"

"If they sent the Immeasurable Man to negotiate with us, then there must be something in here that they want. I say we hear him out...see if we can finagle a get out of jail free card."

"Yeah...okay." The robber unlocked the padlock holding the chain tight around the handles of the outer doors of the vestibule, opened one door slightly, reached an arm out to grab the case, and then relocked the chain. "I'll take the case back to the office while you keep an eye on the hostages and the front door."

As the robber walked along the tile, carrying the case down at his side, IM's holographic figure levitated horizontally above the heads of the prone hostages. Several of them raised their heads off the floor to look at IM. "Stay calm...I'm here to help you...this ordeal will soon be over."

The robber opened the door to the manager's office and entered.

"What the hell?" gasped the manager, looking up from the carpeted floor.

IM muted his channel to the case and addressed the others on the party line. "The manager is alive. Repeat, the voice you just heard matches the vocal recognition the bank's security system has on file. The body growing colder in the corner of the room that my case's thermal sensor is picking up must be that of one of the robbers, as they're the only other two to have been captured on camera entering the office." IM unmuted the case's channel. "So to whom do I have the pleasure of speaking?"

The robber set the case on the manager's desk. "Sure, do you want our social security numbers too?"

"Point well taken. I was only attempting to be polite, but names aren't important now."

The bank manager raised his head again. "I didn't think you'd be so tall."

"Shut up and put your head back down or I'll blow it off," ordered the robber who'd brought IM into the office.

"If it would put any of you more at ease, you're welcome to adjust my height with the knob on the side of the case," said IM.

"I set you up on a desk—that's why you look so tall." The robber took off his suit jacket to reveal a basketball jersey underneath. He positioned the jacket around the case to cover its sides and most of the top, except for the lens that projected the hologram. "I believe that you can't see us, but I'm doing this in case your case has any little peephole cameras the cops stuck on it."

"Doing what?" asked IM.

The gunman tasked with keeping an eye on the hostages appeared in the office doorway. "What's going on?"

"I thought you were watching the front door."

"I can see it and all the hostages just fine from here." The gunman looked at the half-shaven and fully dead robber slumped in the corner. "Jesus, Dylan's seen better days."

IM muted his channel to the case once more. "I assume you all heard that and are now searching your criminal databases for a 'Dylan.'" He studied his screen for a moment. "I see the details coming through for a felon with a matching modus operandi who has a deaf brother named Arlo." He unmuted his case channel. "Is one of your colleagues in need of medical attention?"

"He's past that now," replied the robber who'd brought him in. "The asshole on the floor shot him with a revolver hidden in his desk. He'd be dead now too, except we know the laws in this state. All we wanted was some money—nobody was supposed to get hurt."

"So what's the offer?" asked the gunman in the doorway.

"Now that I know the bank manager is still alive, and if you promise not to harm anyone, you are free to leave. There's a certified letter in this case to that effect, signed by the governor—simply walk out with the paper in hand...hold it up for the news cameras that are no doubt waiting outside, if you like."

"Sounds too easy." The robber moved next to Arlo, who was still seated in the wingback chair, though now melancholy and beardless.

"Would you prefer it to be more difficult?" asked IM.

"No," replied the gunman in the doorway, "more profitable. The way I figure it, the only reason you're here is because there's something more valuable than money in this bank."

Arlo sat up slightly as he noticed IM's twitching hand. "That's very perceptive of you. In the bank's vault there is a safety deposit box that contains documents, which could prove embarrassing for some very powerful people. While you might be tempted to search for those documents yourself, there are a few things to consider. One, the vault houses over a thousand safety deposit boxes, each of which requires a bank key and a matching customer key to open. Two, the vault was remotely locked when the bank's alarm was triggered, and so now the vault door's time lock has been activated, meaning even if you did manage to negotiate for the combination, no one but the Hulk or perhaps the Human Torch would be capable of opening that door for several hours. Three, the documents have no monetary value, though certainly you could attempt to blackmail those who the documents incriminate, but as I mentioned...they're powerful people for whom, I suspect, being extorted would not sit well."

As IM spoke, with his hands down at his side, he signed in ASL letters: ARLO YOUR COMPANIONS WILL NEVER LEAVE THIS BANK FREE MEN. THEY ARE DOOMED TO DIE #UST LIKE YOUR BROTHER DYLAN UNLESS YOU DO AS I TELL YOU. THIS CASE CONTAINS A SONIC DEVICE THAT WILL MOMENTARILY INCAPACITATE ANYONE WITHIN EARSHOT EXCEPT YOU WHO WILL ONLY FIND ITS EFFECTS SOMEWHAT DI**YNG. SHOOT YOUR COMRADES WHEN IT IS ACTIVATED AND YOU HAVE MY WORD THAT YOU CAN FLEE THE BANK DISGUISED AS A HOSTAGE AS YOU HAD PLANNED. OTHERWISE YOU AND YOUR COMRADES WILL BE KILLED BY THE SWAT TEAM THAT INTENDS TO BREACH THE BANK IN LESS THAN FIVE MINUTES WHICH WILL BE FAR MESSIER AND LIKELY RESULT IN COLLATERAL DAMAGE THAT WILL BE ON YOUR HEAD.

"Can we keep the money?" asked the robber standing next to Arlo.

"Of course not," answered IM.

"Then no way," said the gunman in the doorway.

"We've got to have something to show for our trouble," added the robber who then noticed Arlo looking up at him. "And the loss of our friend."

"Give me a moment to confer with the authorities outside." IM left the channel open as he typed the words "disregard inquiry" on his touch screen. "They're asking to keep some of the money...okay, I'll inform them." IM made a clicking noise with his tongue. "If it will help expedite a resolution, you'll be allowed to leave with half."

"Half?" asked the gunman in the doorway.

"What are we supposed to do?" asked the robber near Arlo. "Count up all the money and then divide it in two...that's not going to be very expeditious."

"Ten night-deposit bags have been spotted outside the office—take five," replied IM. "Any five you wish. I assure you, everyone outside—just as I imagine everyone inside—wants all this over with. No one's going renege on the deal over a few extra dollars if you happen to take the five fullest bags."

The gunman in the doorway eyed the zippered bags stacked just outside the door, a few bulging more than the others. He nodded to Arlo and the other robber. "Okay, let 'em know we'll take the deal, but we're walking out of here with a hostage each until we get to those reporters outside and show them the paperwork signed by the governor."

"That's not necessary," said IM, "but so long as no harm befalls them it won't alter the deal."

The gunman in the doorway moved into the office and stood over the manager on the floor. "All right, get up. I pick you as my hostage, and if they start shooting I'll make you my shield."

"We'll take a couple from out there." The robber put a hand on Alro's shoulder.

"Don't forget your paperwork," said IM as he signed in ASL letters: ARLO COUGH SO THAT I KNOW YOU UNDERSTAND AND AGREE TO OUR DEAL.

The gunman pulled the bank manager off the floor by his coat collar and noticed IM's hand. "What's with your fingers? Why're they twitching like that?"

"Yeah," said the other robber. "I noticed that earlier too."

"I'm not sure, since I can't see myself, but it's likely a glitch in the holographic software," replied IM. "It sometimes struggles to fully render extremities."

Arlo coughed. The robber patted him on the back. "There's no reason to get choked up now...we're almost out of here." The robber smiled as he approached the holographic image standing atop the desk. "Just between us, are you really real?"

"I assume you're referring to that persistently circulating conspiracy theory that I'm merely some sort of artificial intelligence," IM said. "You've seen me periodically in interviews over the past few years, correct? I've aged, haven't I?"

The gunman stopped as he led the bank manager toward the office door. "But if you were CGI in the first place, then it wouldn't be no big thing to make you look a little older each year."

"That's an interesting point," said IM, "but I suggest we put this discussion in abeyance for the time being. My authenticity shouldn't concern you right now—only that the letter within this case is, indeed, authentic."

The robber removed his jacket from around the case. "How do I open this damn thing?"

"Just pull that knob I mentioned."

~ * ~

IM heard the familiar chime and looked up at the viewscreen from his protein shake. "Hello there."

"The father of the anonymous bank customer would like to thank you in person for a job well done."

"You mean he's so grateful that he intends to fly all the way to my secluded domicile and risk vectoring in pathogens in an effort to express his appreciation?" asked IM.

"No, I mean he wants to thank you virtually...but in real time."

"Please inform the senator that his unspoken gratitude is thanks enough."

"How did you know he's a...oh, never mind."

"So what happened to the deaf assailant after he shot his associates?"

"The cops corralled all the hostages as they came running out of the bank, so you didn't lie to him, which I know—for reasons I can't fathom—is important to you...he was able to egress just as he'd planned, but the manager IDed him soon after. He didn't do such a great job of shooting his comrades—got them both in the belly...neither died, but at least he incapacitated them, preventing a potential shootout, most likely saving their lives."

"I suppose all's well that ends well." IM returned his attention to his shake.

"I didn't know you knew ASL."

"Just the alphabet—I find it handier than Morse Code."

"Listen, word of your involvement in this incident was leaked to the press, and they've been breathless about it for the past several hours."

"I thought the whole point of my involvement was to keep the incident from becoming a national headline."

"Nevertheless, the media has now taken to portraying you as sort of digital-age Sherlock Holmes...a new hat they seem anxious for you to wear."

"I wear plenty of hats already; I don't want to don a deerstalker too," IM replied. "Besides, I'm like the opposite of that character. He was a sociopathic genius, and I'm just a guy brimming with empathy who happens to have a high-speed Internet connection."

"Be that as it may, I thought I'd give you a heads up, as it seems you haven't been watching the news since your involvement in said incident."

"I got caught up in a Buster Keaton retrospective." IM shook his prepackaged shake container. "Anyhow, it doesn't really matter—it's not likely that reporters will be showing up on my doorstep. By the way, break a leg during your interview tonight. I'll be watching."

Wes Payton has a B.A. in English/Rhetoric/Philosophy and an M.A. in English. He has been a short-story presenter for the Illinois Philological Association. His play *Way Station* was selected for a Next Draft reading in 2015, and *What Does a Question Weigh?* was selected for a staged reading as part of the 2017 Chicago New Work Festival. He is the author of the novels *Lead Tears, Darkling Spinster, Darkling Spinster No More, Standing in Doorways, Raison Deidre, Intimate Recreation, Oblong, The House Painter and the Pirate Hunter, Downstate Illinois, Immurdered: Some Time to Kill, Dissimiles: More's the Pity, Namastab: Transition into Decompose,* and *Jackassignation: Too Clever by Half.* Wes and his family live in Oak Park, Illinois. You can find out more about his work at: http://wespayton.weebly.com/